FOLKLORE

An Adaptation Of Xai & Sia
A Hmong Folklore
From The Oral Story Of Kia Lee
Written & Illustrated by Bao Xiong

MOTH HOUSE

PRESS

ISBN: 978-1-954010-00-0

For my mother, Kia Lee. Thank you for your stories.

CONTENTS

PROLOGUE

A *thousand years before our story begins…*
Heavy gray clouds hung over the land. There was lightning in the far distance, striking pink and blue rays among the dark skies. The rooster's crow signaled the sunrise. A small, gated property sat on a hilltop overlooking the quiet, old village below. A modest wooden house and a barn sat inside the small gated property. The glow from the fireplace lit up the windows and doorway of the house.

Lee and her identical twin sister, Neng, hugged each other. The only thing different about them was the color of their hair; Neng had a long, fine, black hair while Lee had light, golden strands. The sisters stood at the front door of the house, bidding each other farewell. Lee had dark circles underneath her eyes, and ashes smeared on her chin and forehead. She wore a dark blue gown tied at the waist with a long sash. Neng dazzled in a deep plum dress embroidered in various shades of violet and lined with ivory pearls. Her small lips and high cheeks were painted the same shade of pink. She was covered in silver from head to toe; as much as she could wear on her neck, arms, and ankles. Her silver headdress was the main attraction, layered with silver coins, symbols, and hundreds of white and ivory pearls. She looked like a queen.

Lee stared at the cheerful expression on her sister's fair, baby face. Neng looked like a child to her, which made Lee realize that they were still too young to be on their own, but something else was bothering Lee. She felt it in her gut that something was wrong. "Do you have to run away with him?" she asked.

"Yes," Neng replied.

Lee took both of Neng's hands. They each wore a matching gold ring on their right hand that hung loosely around their thin fingers. The face of the rings was shaped like a diamond; with a foreign symbol in the middle. "Talk to father and mother again," said Lee. "They could change their minds when they return."

"No. They forbid me to see him."

"Our parents are just being protective. We don't know his family."

"He's an orphan. They would rather have me marry the wealthy dressmaker's son."

"Everyone here is somewhat wealthy. We live in the trade village. Everyone makes and sells something. Pick another man," suggested Lee, half teasing Neng.

"I love Blong. I have to follow my heart, like you. You can mold silver into anything, and you're good at it."

"But I'll never see you again."

"I'll write you letters. And over the years, maybe our parents won't be angry anymore. Then we can see each other again."

This was all wrong, and Lee felt it in her heart. She hesitated, and then responded with, "I shall miss you."

"I'll miss you every day." Neng hugged Lee again. "I'm so heavy, I feel like I'll fall over. Are you certain you want to give me all your silver?"

"Yes." Lee stepped back to get a good look at her sister. "It's a gift, so you'll never forget me—because I obviously wore them better."

Both girls giggled.

"I'll always remember you. You're my older sister, after all." Tears filled Neng's eyes. "It's time, I must go. He's waiting for me."

Lee reminded her, "Stay out of the woods at night. Remember the things grandmother Pa Kou taught us."

"I know, and I will."

"Safe journey."

"Let us meet again," said Neng. She was hopeful.

"Let us meet again," sighed Lee, sadly.

Moments later, Lee stood at the doorway and watched her sister go to a man, the one who was taking her away, at the end of their property, where two roads crossed paths. Neng turned back to wave at Lee one last time. Tears fell from Lee's eyes as she waved back to Neng.

The fog lifted from the ground, thinning and fading in the soft sunlight. The people in the village below were waking up, lighting their homes, and opening their small shops. Hot steam rose from the rooftops of restaurants and escaped through the open windows, where hungry children stopped to smell the food. The streets were soon filled with traveling merchants, meat and fish markets, and families greeting one another. Suddenly, the trade village no longer seemed like a sleepy old world.

The sun set quickly that day, and a thunderstorm approached with a harsh wind. Neng and her lover rushed hand in hand to the nearest property. It was a small farm where most of the livestock were locked indoors. They entered a small shelter lined with golden hay and buckets of grain. Both of them were soaked from their dark hair to their muddy shoes.

"Wait here. I'll talk to the owners," Blong instructed.

Neng responded with a nod. Blong gave her a devilishly handsome smile and then dashed away. The front door was left open, and the storm poured in. Neng took a step backwards to stay out of the rain. It was dark, damp, and cold inside the shelter. She shivered, rubbing her arms to keep warm. She breathed into her hands and glanced at the gold ring on her right hand. Soon she heard footsteps splattering in the mud outside. It was Blong, and he hurried through the door balancing a tray of items in his muscular arms.

Neng waited patiently for her lover to secure the front door. He turned around with a tray of food and a lamp. The fire from the lamp gave just enough light for them. They settled down on a bed of hay.

"Blong, what did they say?" Neng asked.

Blong gave her a charming smile and replied, "The owners said we can stay here for the week for the price of your silver bracelet. I told them we'll be on our way in the morning. They gave us rice cakes, honey, and tea." Blong took Neng's hand and gently wiped them with a dry cloth. His hands were rough compared to hers. Even in the dim light, she could see the calluses on his palms. Blong had a darker skin tone than Neng, which was also why he admired her flawless face and hands.

They settled down in front of the tray of food. Blong served Neng hot tea, smiling at her happily. Neng smiled back, then she shyly looked away at the rising steam from the tea. Blong couldn't stop staring at her, admiring her beauty and glamor. After the small meal, the lovers lay facing each other on a thin blanket over a bed of hay. The lamp above them bounced soft yellow light off their cheeks and glittered in their eyes as they stared at one another.

"I'm so happy right now," Blong said joyfully. "I want to give you the world."

"I don't want the world. I'm happy with you," said Neng.

Blong paused. He felt nervous as he said, "I love you."

"I love you."

"Would you allow me to finally touch you?"

She was hesitant. "I'll be your bride after tomorrow."

"Yes, but right now...I am at your mercy. I am your creature. Your slave."

Neng stood up abruptly, afraid of what would happen next. Her heart was racing, and she had to be true to herself. "Forgive me, but I cannot allow myself to be yours until we're married."

Blong got up and stood behind her. "There is no one before and no one after you," he said desperately. "How can I prove myself to you?"

"You make me blush."

"My words are true. I'll make you a promise. A new and true promise, with my blood." Blong sounded serious. "Will you honor the same promise with a drop of your blood as well?"

"You're making a very strange proposal, Blong."

"What is truer and more precious than a drop of blood?" Blong took out a small hunting knife from his coat and pricked the pad of his index finger. It bled crimson red. "I'm ready to give myself to you. Body and soul. Here and now."

Neng felt compelled to give in. She extended her hand to him. Blong pricked her index finger and kissed her wound, licking away the bead of deep red blood that came from it. Then he dabbed her rosy bottom lip with the blood from his finger. She sucked on his wound to stop the bleeding.

Blong said, "Now we belong to each other, forever." He leaned in to kiss her cheek.

Neng shut her eyes nervously. She remained still and gave herself to him.

Dawn approached. The cool blue light leaked through the cracks of the wall. The lamp had died out. Neng and Blong slept in each other's arms. Neng was modestly dressed with her shoulders and arms exposed, while Blong laid shirtless in the hay. His long black coat covered them like a blanket. Other pieces of clothing were folded and set to the side, along with the heavy silver jewelry and their shoes.

Suddenly, the front door burst open. An older woman stood over them. She appeared overdressed for the cold, with a touch of old tradition and class. Her skin was tan. She had one hand on her large swollen belly. "This is the girl you're courting?" She spoke with authority, and showed her disgust toward the young beauty that surpassed her own. Her jealousy was easy to read within her disapproving expression.

Neng was shocked and equally embarrassed. She asked, "Who are you?"

Blong raised his voice at the pregnant woman, "SUE—"

"I'm his wife, Sue," said the pregnant woman. She didn't lose her temper or her class.

"You're married," Neng said to Blong with a shaky voice. She was horrified.

"You're not the first girl," said Sue.

Tears streamed down Neng's face. She was lost for words. Ashamed. Humiliated. Betrayed.

"My husband can be most charming," said Sue. "You're young and naive. I forgive you, but you cannot marry my husband. I refuse to share him, even if men can have many wives."

"Get out," Blong said, staring his wife down. "Leave!"

Sue showed no emotion. "If you marry her, you cannot live in my house. You will lose the land and the cattle because my father owns everything, not you. And you will never see your children. You will have nothing, Blong, which is fitting for the orphan you are."

Blong hated those words. He shut his eyes wishing he could shut out his wife.

Sue chuckled. "We cannot even afford hired help; we won't be able to afford a second wife. Look at her," Sue stared at Neng's collection of fine silver set to the side. "You cannot pay her dowry. Were you going to trade her own silver to pay for it?"

"Stop! Stop talking, please," Blong pleaded. He looked ashamed, and he avoided eye contact with Neng.

Sue was satisfied. "Come home, husband," she said, then she stepped out of the shelter. There was a carriage with two dark horses waiting outside. Sue climbed into the front of the carriage. There was no driver. Sue seemed to have driven out to find her husband on her own. Blong couldn't look Neng in the eyes. He gathered his coat and shoes, then he hurried out of the shelter without a word. Neng stayed, frozen. Every fiber of her being was in shock. Tears fell from her eyes, but she was more angry than brokenhearted.

Thunder, lightning, and rain. The storm was still raging that day, pouring over the trade village and the property on the hilltop where Lee sat combing her hair with a silver comb that had long, fine teeth. She stared aimlessly at the wall by the window, lost in her thoughts. A figure approaching the house startled her, and the comb suddenly broke in half and cut her hand. Lee flinched from the pain. She looked at the broken comb in her bleeding palm. *Strange.*

"Bad omen," Lee said out loud.

Her blood spilled over the counter and stained a set of pearls and silver jewelry.

The figure grew closer, and the light from inside the house shone on Neng. Lee dropped the pieces of the silver comb. She rushed to open the front door, and she instantly felt the sadness Neng was going through; it was a sharp stab to her chest. The twins had always shared an emotional connection. Neng looked broken, soaked from the rain, and she appeared to have been crying for some time. She kept her eyes cast down to the ground, ashamed and afraid to look at Lee.

Lee pulled Neng into the warm house right away and embraced her sister. Neng crumbled. Lee felt her sister's body shake and it seemed to shatter with pain.

She spoke softly to Neng, "You're home." Lee took a good look at Neng and brushed away her tears.

Then Lee shut the door. She led Neng to the table near the fire, and gently sat Neng down in front of a plate of exotic fruits next to a small silver-plated knife. She went to the kitchen and put together a pot of tea and two plates of hot food.

Lee carried the tray of food back to the table, but Neng was gone. The table was covered with the silver jewelry that she had been wearing earlier. The front door was left cracked open. Lee abandoned the tray on the table and ran out the door. Her eyes scanned the area, but her sister was nowhere in sight.

Where could Neng have gone at this hour?

The fear inside Lee was gut-wrenching. She wanted to run after her sister, but then she saw the pitch-black woods, and they scared her. Unusual sounds came from the dark forest, sounds not of animals nor humans. Lee stepped back towards the house.

The storm continued. At the top of a bare hill with only one living tree upon it stood Neng. The dark woods stretched out all around her. Some of the trees even looked like trapped and demented bodies. She held a small silver knife in one hand, and the gold ring in her bloody palm.

Lightning struck the tree in front of her, splitting it down the middle. Sparks and fire. The tree burst into flames. A black figure stepped out from the burning tree, naked and dripping with a dark sweat. Steam rose from his chiseled body. He was larger than most men, with jet-black eyes, and he looked more like a creature than a man. The ground burned beneath his feet. Neng knew that this being was not human, but something as old as the earth. Its name was at the tip of her tongue. She felt drawn to the spirit, as if they knew each other.

The ancient spirit spoke with a strong, heavy voice, "You summoned me."

Neng trembled at the sound. She reached her shaking hand out, showing the ring in her bleeding palm. "I've always known you were real." Her voice fluttered. "I want to make a trade."

"The price is your life, body, and soul. My bride," said the ancient spirit.

"You can have me, if you grant all my wishes."

The ancient spirit seemed to like her determination. He was most excited to know about her selfish desires, which were riddled with grief and revenge. He peered deep into her eyes, and simply said, "Name them."

"I want power. More power than you have ever granted to any bride you've taken. I want to create a curse, a drop of blood between lovers that will always end in misfortune or death. And I want to collect the souls of men. Any man I want, starting with Blong Lor."

The ancient spirit replied, "I accept the trade." It extended its muscular arm out to Neng. "You will have everything you asked for, my bride."

Never had Neng been more certain of herself than in that moment. She touched his hand with her fingertips, accepting his offer. The flesh of her fingers sizzled as she touched his burning skin. She flinched and then quickly adjusted to the pain. The ancient spirit grinned and placed the gold ring onto Neng's left hand, burning every piece of flesh he touched. Neng welcomed the torment.

The ancient spirit led Neng to the smoldering charcoal tree. Together, they sank into the body of the dead wood.

The next morning, when the rose-red sun had risen over the horizon and painted the sky pink, Lee finally had the courage to leave the house. A thin layer of fog moved in the air. She fastened the thick, red cloak around her shoulders and took the path away from the property. She soon found muddy footprints in the road. She stepped her right foot into one, like a mold, and it was a perfect fit.

Neng has been here.

After a short while walking on the path, Lee saw that the footprints led into the woods. She quickly entered them, paying attention to her surroundings. The woods were a grove of short, dark barks and branches in a dense, mossy forest. The cawing crows startled Lee, as she hurried alongside the path of the footprints with the wind blowing her golden hair into her face.

Lee arrived at the hilltop and found the scorched tree. Her eyes were filled with horror and tears poured from them.

Neng's body lay in the center of the divided black tree, as if she were sleeping. She was pale and blue. Her lips were black as night, as if she had been kissed by darkness.

Lee let out a horrid cry that echoed through the air.

CHAPTER 1
DEATH

Thousands of years ago, when the stars were young, in the times of gods and demons, old magic and ghostly encounters, the spirits were envious of humans, and fate often tested lovers. All the odds were against Xai and Sia, two lovers compelled to go on a very miraculous journey.

The story began with a wedding. Half-a-dozen wooden carriages traveled on a dirt path through a thick forest. Xai and Sia were dressed in black and red attire, dripping with silver accents as they rode in an open wooden carriage. The horses pulling them were both white, except the one in front of Sia was fairer and more decorated. In front of Xai and Sia were two people who shared a similar-sized carriage, and who were dressed almost identically to them—the groomsman and the bridesmaid. They had also been gifted with a chest of silver bricks and jewelry. The rest of the wedding guests and family traveled in smaller carriages behind the newlyweds.

Xai and Sia had both turned twenty the week they were wed. They mirrored one another: fair skin, peachy lips, kind brown eyes and pitch-black hair. Even their names were similar.

1

On the path to his village, Xai noticed the bridesmaid trying to hide her tears while the groomsman scanned the woods nervously. Xai leaned towards his young wife and asked, "What's wrong with the bridesmaid and groomsman? They seem unhappy."

Sia leaned closer and said, "You don't know? They've been like that since we left the wedding from my mother's house. They're afraid."

"Afraid of what?" asked Xai.

Sia looked around and then lowered her voice. "Spirits."

"Why?"

"Bridesmaids and groomsmen are decoys for evil and vengeful spirits that often snatch a bride or a groom. That's why they lead the way ahead of the bride and groom. It's tradition," explained Sia. "Don't be afraid, it's just superstition."

"Did you tell the bridesmaid about the superstition?"

"She stayed with me for days. We ran out of things to talk about."

"It's also her responsibility to watch you, so other men won't steal you away. She can't do that if she's in hysterics."

"She did very well. She never left my side, not even when I was bathing," said Sia, jokingly.

"Well, you have thoroughly scared her. She must have told my groomsman. Look at him, he's paranoid," said Xai.

The groomsman looked fearfully over his shoulder.

"The bridesmaid is crying," Sia pointed out. "Why are they suddenly more terrified than before? They weren't like that when we traveled through the mountains."

"We're close to the village. The locals say these woods are home to the spirits," said Xai. "Folklore around here is full of cautionary tales, and the people believe in them. So, we keep out of these woods."

"You don't believe in them?" asked Sia.

"They could just be stories," said Xai. He glanced over his shoulder to check on his parents in the carriage behind them.

Xai's parents, an older couple in their sixties, shared a carriage with an elderly couple. They also seemed to be afraid of the forest. There was not a single happy face, just people stealing silent, awkward glances at each other before gazing back down to their own laps. They were afraid to look up.

"I don't understand how an old ghost story can keep elders and villagers out of an entire forest," said Xai. "Surely the spirits of the dead cannot wield such power over the living?"

"You may be right, but some of the stories are true," said Sia.

Xai turned back to his wife. "Did you hear this from someone you know?"

"Yes," replied Sia. "Someone I knew."

Xai looked surprised. His wife smiled at him.

"Well, I don't like to believe in too much talk or tale, it builds fear. Stories and superstitions never scare me, and I have no room for fear today."

"Is it because we were married today?"

"Yes, and I promise you a full life together."

"How long is a full life?" asked Sia.

"One-hundred and twenty years, as they say."

"And who said that?"

"Our ancestors." Xai was confident.

"Our ancestors?" Sia seemed to be testing him. *Does he really know what he's talking about?* she thought to herself.

"Yes, the ones we honor and call home once a year," teased Xai.

Sia didn't answer him.

"It's tradition to honor them."

"I'm aware of that. I've never prayed to them though. I don't know if they really watch over us and protect us."

"You must be the first," said Xai. "I believe in them. Everyone does."

"You don't believe in spirits, but you believe in deceased family members?" she teased him.

Xai chuckled. "And you believe in folklore and superstitions, yet you don't believe in those who came before us. You have to put trust in something. If not ancestors, then what?"

"I've never had to put my trust in anyone before I met you," said Sia.

"Well then, I give you all of my trust. My heart. Everything I am and everything I own."

"A husband entrusting everything to his wife. We will be the envy of the world."

"People will be envious of your horse as well." He looked to the decorated white horse in front of Sia. The horse was furry, with shaggy hair on all four legs leading down to pearl hooves and a snow-like mane and tail. "Try to not ride him in the village; it's frowned upon, and people will talk."

"I shall try my best. Dawb (Der) likes to go for runs. Sometimes I let him go out on his own; he knows his way home."

That surprised him. "You named your horse?"

"Don't you have names for yours? How do you call them?"

"We just call them," said Xai. "The villagers share these horses. Everyone uses them, and everyone takes care of them. It's always been that way."

"Interesting village."

They finally cleared the woods. The new scenery lit up Sia's face.

Xai glanced at her, and caught her delighted expression. "Welcome home."

His words and the thought of the lovely home ahead gave Sia more reasons to smile.

They had reached a large red oak tree at the far end of the village. The red oak was already home to a black, crow-like bird.

The location was private and spacious, away from the rest of the vibrant village that lay nestled at the foothill of a mountain.

Their home was built out of bamboo, which was a willowy green color. It was a humble hut with a gated yard, full of brown piglets and fluffy chickens. Dawb, the serene white horse was the perfect addition.

There's joy on everyone's face. Xai's parents were glad to be home, and the wedding party were all relieved to have arrived at their destination safely. They parked the carriages outside of the gated property and helped the newlyweds move into their new home.

The couple soon grew comfortable in their new roles as husband and wife. The elegant horse greeted them daily when they returned home after tending to their small vegetable garden and rice field. The hunting, gathering, and farming tools they used were all handsomely crafted by the young couple, mostly carved out of wood and molded metal.

Most days, Xai would start the fire with logs of wood while his wife prepared the meals. They'd eat in perfect harmony. The sweet, starchy taste of fresh steamed rice would melt in their mouths and fill their bellies. Each time their eyes met, they blushed from shyness, but it was joy like no other. Late at night, she'd brush her fingers through his dark, straight hair, while he told her tall tales handed down from his parents and grandparents. She'd breathe in the clean scent of his washed and damp hair while falling asleep next to him.

Other than friendly greetings in the village, the people kept to themselves. Xai's parents joined them for breakfast every once in a while, and his parents always reminded them to keep out of the woods and return home before dark.

Then, one day, there was a minor disturbance in the village. The elders kept the matter quiet, but the whispers from people about the mysterious death of a young man from one of the houses in the village soon reached Sia. Days after this disturbing incident, Xai's parents came to breakfast. All four of them ate silently, but Sia was burning with questions.

"Did anyone hear about the recent incident and the young man who died?" asked Sia.

Xai stayed silent, but his facial expression showed that he knew more about it than he was letting on.

"It's nothing to worry about," said Xai's father. He had finished eating, and stood up.

"We'll go to the farm after father and I gather some wood," Xai told Sia. He got up and followed his father out the front door.

The men took an ax and a long knife.

Sia asked her mother-in-law, "Would you tell me why the women are saying there's a demon in the woods?"

"The elders tried to keep that matter quiet, but the women here like to talk. Their whispers have clearly reached you," said Xai's mother, accusingly.

"Tell me what happened to that man," implored Sia.

Xai's mother was hesitant. She glanced out the front door to make sure no one else was around. Then she lowered her voice. "This was not the first incident. Men had gone hunting or traveling, and they would return home sick. Some men reported hearing voices of women in the woods. Others reported seeing strange things among the trees, such as shapeshifters. The illness is unusual, with a fever and a cold sweat, but also with delusions and strange talk." She paused. This next part was difficult for her to say. "They all died. Most healers are afraid to travel to our village. This has been a normal occurrence for the villagers for centuries, and the people carry on with their lives because that is all they can do. Like you, I had to adjust to living here."

"The woods really are haunted," said Sia.

"And your farm is right by them," said Xai's mother. "That's why Xai's father and I remind you both to stay out of it. We dislike talking about the spirits around here."

"Forgive me for being curious." Sia suddenly felt anxious. Her right hand trembled, so she clasped it firmly with the other hand.

Xai's mother saw her hand shaking. "I didn't mean to scare you. Don't tell Xai, he doesn't like to believe in these things. That's why he didn't mind purchasing this land along with the farm. No one else wanted a property so close to the woods."

"Did the previous owner live here too?"

"No. It was just a plot of land. My son built this home for you and him."

Sia smiled on that note.

Xai's mother handed Sia a necklace made of red fabric, hung with a hand-sewn charm. The charm was triangular-shaped, stuffed, and had red and green Hmong symbols stitched on both sides.

"It's to ward off nightmares," said Xai's mother. "Xai told us that you've been having many nightmares since you came here. Wear it to sleep."

"Thank you," said Sia, as she took the necklace. Looking at the hand-sewn charm made Sia miss her mother. "My mother used to make these for us," said Sia.

"You live far from your mother now; you must miss her."

"I miss her very much."

"A mother will always miss her child," said Xai's mother.

Her words brought comfort to Sia.

"What is inside?" asked Sia, holding up the charm. Her fingers rubbed on what felt like tiny items the size of rice and corn inside the charm.

"Medicine."

"What kind of medicine?"

Xai's mother leaned toward Sia and lowered her voice. "A few secret ingredients I cannot speak of, and words."

Sia wanted to learn more about it. "Why are words used in this charm?"

"Charms should be enchanted with words, otherwise they'll just be another item, and useless."

Sia grew more curious. "What kind of words?"

"My own words, to banish bad dreams." Xai's mother explained, "Words are powerful. They can bring change, healing, and curses. So, be careful how you speak."

"I'll remember that."

"Shall we head out to the farm?"

"Yes."

Xai's mother picked up her plate. Sia got up from her chair and helped her with clearing the table.

Later that night, Sia and Xai sat on a blanket by the fire. He fed wood into the flames while she stitched a shirt. He took the shirt and needle away from her hands and set them aside.

"You need the shirt for tomorrow," said Sia.

"You've worked all day. Perhaps we can just sit here, and do nothing," he suggested.

She liked that idea. "Do nothing?"

"Or, anything you want." He opened his arms to her. Sia went to his arms and laid on his chest. He pulled the blanket over her, and as he did so, he felt the nightmare charm around her neck. He touched the charm.

"Let's hope this keeps away the bad dreams," said Xai.

"Especially the recurring one."

"You're having the same dream more than once? Perhaps it's a sign."

"We're standing in the fog, and there's a woman following us." She looked at him. "What does that mean?"

"I'm not sure. How many times have you had this dream?" he asked.

"Three times."

"Don't worry over a dream."

"But I feel scared."

"Now?"

"In the dream. I'm scared when she's there."

"Don't be scared. It's just a dream. You can wake up, and that'll be the end of it."

"Lately, I've been afraid to fall asleep."

He hugged her. "I'll be right here. Now, get some sleep."

"Are we sleeping by the fire tonight?"

"If that is what you wish."

"The light makes me feel safe."

"You're safe with me, wife." His words comforted her, and she closed her eyes.

"Tell me a story," said Sia, tired, and sleepy.

"You're like a child."

"Tell me a story," she repeated.

"A long, long time ago…" His voice faded as she fell fast asleep.

The day their quiet and charming life changed began with a normal, daily routine. The couple was working in the garden near the haunted woods. The sun was exceedingly hot, filling the air with shimmering heatwaves. Xai, who was digging a hole with a long gardening tool, had to stop for a moment. He leaned on the wooden stick of the gardening tool for support, defeated and dehydrated in the heat. His clothes stuck to his skin. He pushed the round bamboo hat off his head and rubbed the sweat from his bushy brows onto the sleeve of his shirt. He breathed deeply.

He looked at his wife. Sia was not far behind him, tossing grains of rice into the row of holes. She stayed low to the ground. The smell of the gritty, rich dirt didn't bother her. She was nimble and graceful, and she enjoyed her work. Her straw hat kept her face shaded.

Xai called to his wife. "Sia, I'm thirsty. Will you bring me some water? I don't know why but I'm thirstier than normal."

Sia raised her head again. Her cheeks had been made rosy by the flaring sun. Xai smiled at the sight of her lovely face. She noticed his chapped lips, and that his hat was slung over his shoulders instead of shading his head. She picked up the light brown gourd from the ground and shook it. It was empty. Suddenly, the gourd cracked under her thumb. It was a bad omen. She inhaled deeply. The uneasy feeling in her chest grew tighter. Sia briefly glanced towards the edge of the haunted forest, which was a few yards away from their garden.

Sia walked towards her husband, who looked exhausted. "We don't have any water left. Do you want to go home?"

"We have more work to do," Xai said, determinedly.

Sia agreed, but she was afraid to leave him alone. "Don't go anywhere. Stay right here," she said. "No matter what you hear, don't go and see what it is. You must wait until I return." She fixed his hat on his head to give him shade.

"Yes," Xai replied, although he wasn't worried.

Sia left him and hurried back to their house for water. It was a short walk to exit the farmland and to find the dirt road that led straight back to their village. Sia soon reached the red oak tree, nearing home. She touched her stomach. Something was wrong, and she felt it in her bones. She started to run toward home. The black bird watched Sia as she ran underneath the red tree.

Sia burst through the wooden gate, and it slammed shut behind her. She avoided the piglets that came to greet her. The white horse nodded at her return. She raced for the little bamboo hut. Her bare feet carried dirt into the doorway.

Sia spotted the wide silver bowl where they kept their water, covered with a white cloth to keep it clean. Dried, pear-shaped gourds hung from the wall above the silver bowl.

Sia snatched the rope that bound two large brown gourds together. They were filled and heavy. She turned around and hurried back towards the field, the water splashing against the walls of the round gourds.

Back at the field, the sound of running water had caught Xai's attention. Desperate to quench his thirst, he followed the noise until he reached a rushing stream flowing with crystal-clear liquid.

"This was not here before," Xai thought. But it didn't matter where the water had come from. It thrilled Xai to find what he needed, and he quickly forgot his unease.

Suddenly, shadows materialized from the trees behind Xai. Ghostly entities, spirits of the departed. Xai was oblivious of the dead as they surrounded him. As Xai scooped up the water with both hands and drank, a dozen red lips lined with tar grinned from the shadows. The moment he swallowed, Xai heard women's laughter, layered with heavy, sinister chuckles that sounded like nothing he'd heard before. He stared around in panic. No one was in sight, only trees and shadows.

Little did he know, the stream of water he had drank from was actually urine from a group of spirits; they had played a wicked and deadly trick on Xai.

"Xai drinks our pee," one spirit declared, "Xai is now our husband indeed."

He heard them speak his name. His shoulders dropped.

Another spirit giggled. "Xai drank our things that are old, he is now our son to hold."

The voices of the dead struck fear in his heart. He could hear it pounding like a drum. A cold wave of shock vibrated through his body, and he turned and fled. He reached the rice field and slumped down in terror. The distress overwhelmed him so much that he had forgotten how the water from the mysterious stream had tasted. *Was it bitter? Was it light and fresh like rainwater? Was it tasteless?* His hands trembled.

Sia arrived at the scene to see her petrified husband, who sat in agitated silence with a spooked, paled face.

She held the gourds of water out towards him. "Xai, I'm here. I've brought water. Come and drink."

"I've already drunk some water."

Sia's stomach turned sour. There was no source of water nearby. "Xai, why didn't you listen to me?"

A strange feeling settled in their stomachs. They stared at each other briefly, not knowing what to do next. Eventually, they went back to work in awkward silence.

After some time, Xai broke the silence. "This year, Xai prepared the land and Sia planted. Xai dug holes while Sia threw in grains. Next year, who will dig holes for Sia to lay seeds?" There was sorrow in his voice. His words only added to the fear of bad omens that lingered in Sia's thoughts.

She glared at him. *Why was he speaking in riddles?* She composed herself and replied, "It'll be you. Who else would I wait for?"

After the couple's work in the field was complete, they gathered their baskets and gardening tools. Side by side, they made the short journey home, just in time for the blood-orange sun to disappear behind the emerald mountains, painting the sky a deep red.

That night, a feast sat untouched on the wooden table inside their bamboo hut. Herbs were layered over a boiled chicken in a clay pot. Small bamboo bowls of soup and chili peppers accompanied charcoaled fish, served on banana leaves. Steam escaped from the pockets between the piled rice, like two hot mountains sitting inside hollowed bamboo. The handcrafted wooden chairs were empty. No one was going to eat this meal.

Xai had suddenly fallen ill. He was as pale as a ghost, tucked in bed under the cover of a woven blanket. It was difficult for Sia to suppress the worry on her face as she washed the dirt from her husband's hands with a wet cloth. A paper lantern sat on a side table next to the bed, illuminating the room. Both of them felt watched by the shadows. They were two scared people, being scared together. Both fearing the worst.

Xai had lost the strength to raise his hand to touch hers. He felt the aching in his bones.

"Sia… when I die, visit me in three days. Bring me breakfast to feast on, hot water to wash my face, my musical instruments, my *qeej* [(K) qang] and my *ncas* [(G) c-ya]. Come to me on the morning of the third day..." Xai spoke his last words, shut his eyes, and died.

Sia didn't have time to answer him. Tears poured from her eyes. She stayed beside her husband, gazing upon him. His beautiful eyes were closed. His pale face seemed at peace, so still. For the first time in her life, Sia felt utterly alone. The cold silence broke her heart.

Her lips parted to whisper, "Too beautiful. Too young for death."

Her hand brushed his forehead and traveled over the top of his head. She recalled the times she had combed her fingers through his hair. The strands were still silky and fine, but he had been warmer then.

Sia began to sob softly, and her sobs soon became agonized crying. She cried for the short time they had had together. She cried for this moment that made her feel like she could die. The pain was a monster, forcing her body to lose every ounce of strength. Sharp stabs at her heart made it beat faster. Clutching her chest, she struggled to breathe. It took her hours to calm down, but she had no control over the tears pouring from her eyes, even when she closed them.

A bead of red streaked down from her closed eyes. The tears had turned to blood.

She stayed on her knees at Xai's side long until the morning. The sunrise was not the same. The sounds of life happening outside were not the same. Nothing felt good anymore. Sia exhaled. It hurt to breathe. She laid her head next to Xai and stayed with him, her fingers locked with his.

CHAPTER 2
THE SPELL

The funeral spanned two days. Family and close friends filled Xai and Sia's humble home. Sia and her family prepared folded boats, painted with silver and gold, intended to be bricks of silver and gold for the afterlife. The village men worked as butchers with the meat, clashing with the group of female cooks. Young men carried wooden buckets of fresh water to the front yard of the hut, while others chopped wood for fire near the cooks. Incense was lit, and two shamans performed rituals, one skilled in playing the drum and the other skilled in playing the *qeej*, to ferry the souls of the dead through their song.

Sia wore the same black and deep purple clothes for the entire duration of her time in mourning. While she honored every funeral tradition, everything was a blur to her. She didn't know how she could continue to live a life without Xai.

Widow. She wasn't used to being called, "Xai's widow." Even as she heard people whispering it in private, the words meant nothing to her.

19

Cooks gathered in the front yard of the hut, surrounded by the steam from the rice cooking. The older women were already deciding Sia's future, as they tasted the scorching, soft rice, and mumbled amongst themselves.

"Married and widowed in less than a year. What will she do now?" asked the eldest woman.

"My brother needs a wife. He has two small children who need a mother," said the youngest woman. "And she's nineteen."

"Sia is twenty years old, like her late husband," another lady corrected.

"I married when I was fifteen," a short, round woman reminded the others. "My daughter just got married last year, and at eighteen years old she was lucky to find someone. It would be a terrible fate to marry an old man."

"What village is she from?" asked another cook.

"No one knows for sure," said the eldest woman. "Perhaps she's an orphan." She tasted the hot rice. "Nevertheless, she's a widow. Sia would be lucky if any man married her now, as a second wife. Talk to your brother."

Sia was carrying a basket of washed, ruby-red apples as she passed by the chattering cooks. The cooks awkwardly fell silent once they noticed her.

"Be respectful. Hold your tongue," Sia whispered under breath, to calm herself down and stop herself from lashing out at the inconsiderate women. *They're here to help*, she told herself.

Her emotions were numb, but she was quietly. Sia desperately needed to be outside, away from the other mourners. She found the placid white horse, and called him by his name, "Dawb." He was a calming presence, good for her sore eyes. She fed Dawb an apple. He ate the fruit from her hand graciously. Sia set the basket of apples on the ground. She stayed with the horse for comfort while she tried to tune out the noise of the guests, from the rude gossiping cooks to the close relatives paying their respects.

A warm, light droplet bounced onto the crown of her head. Rain. People ran around in dismay, gathered their things, and scattered to the nearest shelters in the village. However, the rain on Sia's skin was refreshing. She welcomed the downpour of the storm. With the sudden rainfall came the scent of heavy clouds, pine trees, and rocks. The earth smelled abundant and alluring. Sia took a deep breath and let go.

It was the next day when Sia was finally able to bathe. She submerged herself under hot water, screaming her grief. Bubbles broke on the surface of the wooden tub. Sia came up for air and gasped.

The quietness and privacy of the shed was a haven. Clean cloth, clothes, and the nightmare charm hung to the side, nearby the tub. The first light broke over the horizon and came through the open window and shined on her face. She shut her eyes against the light.

Sia's in-laws arrived at the house, just a few feet away. She could hear them talking to the guests. Sia tilted her head back and relaxed. *Just one more minute.* The dark circles under her eyes felt sore. She inhaled the steam, and then reached for the long cloth that hung on the side.

Moments later, Sia put on a fine dress, but not so fine as to offend anyone in mourning. The dress had just the right amount of hand-detailed embroidery to complement the deep red fabric: pictures of coiled snails and the stair-steps of a house. She pinched the dress at her chest and secured it with a silver needle that had a rosy pearl on one end. Then she tied the burgundy sash firmly at her slim waist. She clipped a silver moth pen in her hair. For the final touches, she added a red, braided bracelet made from torn fabric and a silver necklace with a spirit lock pendant. The spirit lock was rectangular-shaped with curled-in snail shells at the top.

Glistening drops of morning dew hung from the crisp green leaves in the trees. The sky cast gray clouds, and the morning was the beginning of a cold, grim day. It would have been an even uglier day if it weren't for the tiny beads of water perfectly balanced on the blades of grass like little spheres of light.

The burial of Xai was on that third morning at sunrise. Sia stood in the front row with her in-laws. People pitied her youth and beauty now that she was a widow, and Sia saw it on their faces. She watched as the last handful of soil was tossed into the grave. The man she had spoken to everyday was now in the earth underneath the mound of fresh dirt. Her grief was nearly driving her mad, but Sia composed herself as grieving family members bade farewell to Xai. Even if she wanted to cry, she couldn't, because her tears had turned to blood, and dried up.

The clan leader reached the end of the burial ritual and the remaining mourners left the plot of graves before the morning dew had fallen off the leaves.

It was finally quiet, and she was finally alone. The gray clouds grew darker and kept the sunlight away, creating a gloomy, dreadful day. Sia brought the items that Xai had requested: a hot meal set in silver bowls, accompanied by a silver cup filled with rice wine, hot water in a silver bowl, and two instruments: Xai's *qeej* and his *ncas*.

Sia laid them out perfectly at the head of the grave. She announced to her husband, "Xai, I've brought you breakfast, hot water, and your *qeej* and *ncas*. Wake up and wash your face, feast, and play the *qeej* and *ncas*."

Sia pretended to leave. Once she had cleared the area, she hid in the bushes and waited. The cool air unexpectedly got colder. She looked to the back of her wrist where the hairs were standing up on their own. Seeing the braided red bracelet gave her a sense of security. The freezing air brought with it a mist, which soon became a thick fog. Sia touched the silver pendant around her neck, which brought her reassurance of protection. She braced herself. All she could hear was the beating of her heart, growing louder and faster. Deep down, she knew something extraordinary was about to happen. *If Xai did not believe in spirits and folklore, then why did he request a last meal after his burial?*

Suddenly, a woman's singing echoed in the air, "Da, der, ler. Da, der, ler. Humans stake the strength, spirits stake to break and end. The soft ground moves right into two piles and bends."

Sia saw nothing, yet her ears heard the inexplicable voice. She began to wonder if she should stay or run. *Was this a spirit?*

The voice continued to speak in riddles. Then, the spirit of a woman floated at the foot of Xai's grave. Sia could not shut her eyes. She couldn't believe what she was seeing. Her teeth chattered, and her entire body shook. This was the most unnatural thing she'd ever seen—a spirit.

The spirit had long strands of silver hair that were slowly turning dark and growing thicker by the second. Her skin looked burnt and decayed, but it was healing by the second. Mahogany stains sullied her once-purple gown, and there were black pearls over the dark embroidery; the black pearls might have been ivory once. On her head sat a black crown draped with a long, sheer veil that covered her face. She looked like the bride of a demon, and she had an ominous aura. Her skeletal arms were raised. On her left hand was a golden ring, diamond-shaped with a seal on the face. Her crooked red lips separated, and she spoke once more.

"Da, der, ler, fall. Da, der, ler, fall. Humans stake to break and end. Spirits stake the strength. The soft ground moves in two directions. Xai awakens!"

It was a spell to bring Xai back from the dead. By this time, the spirit had miraculously regenerated some solid features with a fully formed face, long dark black hair, and skin. She had claws at the tips of her fingers, like a wild animal. Her skin was still decaying on the surface in random patches, but she was strikingly beautiful. She looked ancient and regal. She possessed the aura of a thousand-year-old soul. Every grain of soil and material that pulled too close to her energy field quickly disintegrated.

The dirt over Xai's grave broke open. Xai rose from the hole in the earth. He stepped out of the grave and shook the dirt off his body. Strong as the day he lived. Stronger now that he was dead.

Sia's eyes widened in astonishment at the sight of her dead husband standing over his own grave. Pale-skinned, dressed in a lavishing red and black robe, Xai stepped forwards, mighty and god-like. Sia had known she would see him again. She gathered her courage and prepared to take action.

The moment his feet touched the cold ground, Xai opened his eyes. He was different. The proof was in his eyes—he had a wider, darker, and lifeless gaze. He washed his face with the water from the large silver bowl, which still gave off some steam from the surface. He ate the food at the head of his grave. It shocked Sia to her core, but she couldn't stop watching him.

He played the *ncas*, three songs for humans and three songs for spirits. He grasped the *qeej* in both hands and played three songs for humans and three more for spirits.

On the last note, Sia leaped from the bushes and firmly locked her arms around her husband's waist.

The spirit was filled with jealousy. "Xai's fat wife," she sneered.

"No. She's just my younger sister," lied Xai. He sounded emotionless.

He turned to face Sia with a cold expression. "Younger sister, why are you here?"

The light in his eyes was no more. No brown irises. Nothingness. Black filled his eyes.

Sia peered into his large black eyes. "Xai, if you live, I live with you. If you die, I die with you. Wherever you go, I'll go too."

Xai stared at her. The look of death on his face did not scare her. She gripped him tightly. Xai knew that she wasn't letting him go.

Suddenly, more figures appeared around Xai and Sia. There were too many spirits for Sia to count. The dead were playing tricks on her human eyes. Four doubled to eight. She saw eleven, which quickly became thirteen. The spirits were dead women, some buried in fine gowns and others in rags. Heads with long black hair that extended to their ankles. Their dried, worn feet did not touch the ground. One of them was missing eyes. Another spirit only had half a face. Some had their damaged faces hidden behind veils, brides who had died on their wedding day. The largest figure among them was an old hag, like the ones from the haunting stories of sleep paralysis; she wore a sinister grin that grew more malevolent by the moment. One spirit appeared centuries older than the demon bride. The spirits' fingernails were dangerously long, like sharp blades. A foul stench followed the spirits. All sickly. All wicked. All deadly.

Xai slowly pulled away from Sia, but she held onto his hand. He locked his fingers between hers.

There were thirteen spirits in all. They made a path for Xai, but his living and breathing wife held his waist firmly. The demon bride was first in line; everything about this entity was darker than the rest, almost demonic.

Sia glued her face to Xai's icy chest. No heartbeat. Sia remembered that her husband was still dead, even though he was standing in front of her. She could see every breath coming out of her mouth, but not his. She was intimidated by many things, but she told herself silently: *I won't be beaten by the freezing cold, not by my dead or undead husband, nor by these spirits.*

Xai smiled at Sia, kind and sincere. Joy lit up Sia's face, and she took the first step with Xai down the aisle of dead, floating women. In front of them stood the forest, thicker and wilder than they'd ever seen it before. It seemed as though the trees were more than just living plants, growing and transforming before their very eyes. Behind them was the world they knew. The couple walked side by side toward the unknown. With each step, Xai and Sia disappeared further into the pitch-black shadows of the woods.

CHAPTER 3
THE DARK WORLD

Sia stayed close to her husband, traveling further into the dark world. The surroundings were a deep gray and blue, containing no sun and no warmth. Sia looked around her. They were not quite in the afterlife, nor were they among the living. The path blurred between the world of the dead and the world of the living.

Sia thought to herself, *Where am I? Is this limbo?* She glanced at the spirits that were still following behind them. The spirits talked among themselves in whispers, their voices jealous and cruel.

"Xai's fat wife is tough," said one spirit, lifting her veil to intimidate Sia with her grisly face.

"She dares follow us into our world," hissed another spirit.

"Then let's take her to feast on chicken stomachs," suggested another spirit.

They all stopped to rest near a path of rocks, where a spring flowed beside them. Xai and Sia kept their distance from the spirits.

"Don't drink the water here," Xai told Sia. "Try not to eat anything."

Sia responded with a nod.

The spirits bashed the shells of water snails and giggled among themselves with ugly faces and trolling laughter. The snails shriveled and rattled out of fear. Crack, crack, crack. The spirits continued to split more spiraled shells away from the sluggish creatures.

Sia was presented with large snails on a bed of two charcoal hands. The black and gray creatures crawled away from each other at the slowest pace. The snails were as big as Sia's head. The spirit leaned closer to Sia, pressuring her to eat.

Sia's hands slowly reached for one, and she hid her anxiety in the only way possible, *just do it*. She opened her mouth and bit down. *Chew. Chew. Chew.* Tears streaked down Sia's powdered cheeks as she swallowed the nasty treat. Slimy mucous covered her face. She gagged.

Evil smiles. Unholy chuckles. The spirits watched in delight as Sia wrestled with herself and the poor slippery snails. Even after Sia had finally swallowed, the snails kept coming. The spirits piled them at Sia's feet. Sia couldn't keep up with the hill of squirming snails before her.

Xai saw that his wife was suffering. He lowered his voice to a whisper, so that only she could hear him, and said, "Sia, toss them behind you."

Sia tossed the snails over her shoulders one by one. She was too busy pretending to pop the snails into her mouth that she didn't see what was happening right behind her. Xai was eating the live snails for her. He devoured every one of them, quick and without a trace. It surprised the spirits to see the pile of snails gone. It upset one spirit, who exclaimed, "Xai's fat wife is resilient!"

"Then let's take her to feast on pickled greens," suggested another spirit.

The spirits led the couple to another location, a land with patches of black mud and rich, damp dirt. The spirits hand-picked earthworms from the dirt and dropped them into Sia's hands. The giant worms wiggled over one another. Again, Sia couldn't stop the tears from reaching her eyes. She was only human. There was suddenly a mound of worms building higher and higher. *How was this even possible?* Sia's face turned sour as she choked on a worm.

Xai pitied his wife. He spoke in a low tone. "Sia, don't cry. Toss them behind you."

Sia noticed that the spirits weren't paying close attention. She remembered what she had done earlier, and she threw the worms over one shoulder when the spirits weren't looking. Sia looked over her shoulder to check on the pile of worms, but there was nothing to see. Xai had consumed the entire mass of worms faster than his wife had discarded them. The spirits were in shock to find that Sia had been able to make the worms disappear.

Sia was thinking about what was to come. *What a sad fate for spirits to linger in such a place. To have to feed on such grotesque things. Do all spirits come here? Will I be stranded here too?* But seeing Xai's face once more, Sia cast away her fears and doubts.

The couple continued their journey. The grim atmosphere became even darker than before. The air thickened. Sia's breath appeared like white fog. She hugged herself for warmth. It was nightfall in this world, or so it seemed. Sia looked to her husband for comfort. He glanced at her from time to time. That was enough for her.

Soon, they arrived in another peculiar land. Tall grass and thick greenery masked the true shape of the area. A cliff that contained an endless black cave appeared. Near this mysterious pit was where Xai stopped walking, so that Sia could rest. The spirits followed his lead without question, and as if he had cast some kind of alluring spell over them—they drew to him wherever he went.

Xai saw that Sia had become sleepy. "I need to sleep, so I can properly rest," Xai said loudly. The spirits became excited.

"I get Xai's front," one spirit said.

"I get Xai's back!" declared another spirit.

Xai interrupted the fighting spirits, "If you all want to be in front of me, then allow my younger sister to be behind me. If you all want the place at my back, then allow my sister the place in front of me."

"Xai loves his fat wife," said an envious spirit. "Then let us claim his front."

The horde of spirits knew about the endless black pit, so they positioned themselves away from the cliff. One spirit pushed Sia toward the cliff's edge. "Your place is here."

Xai instantly got between them. The spirit left Sia alone. Xai laid down next to Sia, with all the spirits settling down to his right side. The rest of the spirits laid their floating bodies to the ground and for a moment shut their eyes as if they were human again, in need of sleep.

Sia whispered to Xai, "Can't we escape them?"

He whispered back, "No. No matter where I go, they'll find me. Especially the one with the gold ring."

Sia remembered that spirit well.

"She raised me from the grave."

"Why?"

"I don't know." Xai's fingers curled in. "I feel chains around my arms, and they are connected to her."

Sia suddenly noticed that he now had fangs. She thought: *first his eyes, and now his teeth. He is changing.*

Many of the spirits placed their claws on Xai, turning his face and body towards them. He stopped talking. Sia's teeth chattered. She quickly bit down and breathed deeply through her nose. The closest spirit to Xai let her guard down, surrendered to his arms, and closed her pure-black eyes.

Sia slumbered at the back of her husband's body. The fog was so thick, she was unaware that she was physically near the edge of the cliff. It was still cold, but Sia was too tired to notice and soon exhaustion took over, and she fell asleep.

Moments later, a spirit somewhere in the middle of the herd of dead women suddenly woke up. The spirit searched for Sia. She stretched her arm all the way across the others and pricked Sia's arm with her sharp-as-knives nails.

Sia jolted awake. Warm blood trickled down her arm. A dozen nostrils of the dead flared, as the spirits caught the scent of open flesh, and soon it became a bloody game. Poked. Punctured. Blood leaked from Sia's stained sleeve. The spirits relentlessly pinched and pricked Sia's arm. Ripped her dress and tore her skin. They marked Sia with multiple wounds. The strong metal scent of her blood woke more spirits.

Sia didn't want the spirits to have the satisfaction of hearing her, so she cried quietly. But she couldn't let this go on. "It's painful, Xai."

Xai whispered, "Sia, it's right in front of you."

Sia glanced down at her dress and saw the silver needle pinned at her chest. It shimmered back at her. Silver, an element that warded off spirits and other supernatural beings. She took the silver needle and waited for the next attack, which came quickly. Sia watched for the long nails to approach her shoulder once more. *JAB!* She stabbed the silver needle into the rotting flesh of the dead woman's hand and burnt a wound into the decaying skin.

The spirit immediately pulled back her injured hand. "Xai's fat wife is tough!"

Sia was amazed to see black tar burning on the silver needle. *Was this from the spirit?* She realized that she could harm spirits with silver. Sia held the silver needle tightly; she was ready to do it again.

The next spirit reached for her, stretching her arm to grab a portion of Sia's flesh. But this time, Sia was ready to return the favor. The long fingers of the dead woman met with the silver needle twice. The spirit took her sizzling hand back and mumbled, "Xai's fat wife!"

Another spirit spread her fingers to Sia's face and met the same fate. *POKE! POKE!* Eventually the spirits caught on to what Sia was doing, and they gave up attacking her.

Soon, everyone dead and alive was sleeping, except for Xai. He waited long enough to make sure the spirits were in a deep sleep before he opened his eyes. The dead could rest in a deep slumber that they could not easily awaken from.

Xai turned to his wife, took her in his arms, and hovered, moving over the sleeping spirits until he and his wife had reached the end of the last sleeper. Xai repositioned his wife, so she was no longer facing the edge of the cliff. Wearing a red dress, Sia blended right in with the rest of the spirits in red at the end of the line. Xai returned to his place near the cave, and placed a random spirit at his back, hoping the others would confuse this one for his wife.

It wasn't long before a spirit somewhere close to Xai awakened and launched a forceful kick at the body closest to the edge of the bottomless pit. Another spirit woke up just in time to witness the body falling off the edge. The two bitter spirits watched the body of a woman in a red dress fall to her doom, and they grinned to one another.

There was a ledge far below, somewhere in the dark pit, where two blind tigers lived. The creatures were suddenly aware that they were not alone. The blind tigers sniffed the scent of the body. Sticky saliva dripped from their fangs. The blind tigers jumped at the spirit and tore her into two pieces. Starved, the blind creatures gobbled her up. The crunching of her bones echoed up the walls of the cave to the top of the cliff.

The spirits smirked to each other and returned to their places. Now that the human was gone, they would sleep well. Discreetly, Xai filled the vacant spot behind him with another snoozing spirit.

Later, a spirit in the middle suddenly opened her eyes, quivering with excitement at her own plan to rid them of Xai's fat wife. She took one look at the body in a red gown laying at the edge of the cliff, and instantly assumed it was the human. The spirit stretched her leg all the way over to the sleeping woman, making her bony foot identical to a long dying tree branch. She gave the body at the edge a great big kick. The body vanished over the cliff and into the pit.

Snatch! The sound of the blind tigers munching on the body's limbs brought pleasure to the spirit. She closed her eyes and planted herself down to rest with a devilish grin. On and on it continued, one spirit after another thinking they had brought the demise of Xai's fat wife.

Hours passed. The darkness had faded. Perhaps it was now daytime in the world of the dead. Sia could see the remaining spirits as they looked around at their much smaller group of dead women, confused as to why there were only half of them left. It enraged the envious spirits to see Xai standing next to Sia. She was still alive after all their efforts to destroy her.

"So Xai's fat wife is resilient," said one spirit.

"Let's see how she fares leaping over the mouths of dragons and tigers," said another spirit.

CHAPTER 4
DRAGONS AND TIGERS

When they arrived at the next point on their journey, Sia was intimidated by the giant rocks the size of mountains that formed many deep valleys. Colossal monsters governed each one: here a dragon, and there an enormous tiger. The beasts clashed heads, unable to escape the invisible barrier between the mountains. There was no way that she could climb them; *it'll be impossible to leap over them.* She was more worried about the monsters in the valleys. It was as though the giant creatures were cast into this cold shadow world and cursed with hunger.

One spirit proudly went first. She leaped from one rock to the next, barely making it to the edge of the cliff. A dragon swung its tail against the monstrous rock, rattling the entire mountain, and the spirit lost her balance. The dragon snatched her out of the air and crunched her in its jaws. It caused an uproar of excitement in the valley; dragons and tigers shoved each other out of the way with their mouths propped open, awaiting any further mistakes from the travelers. The next arrogant spirit made a great jump, but she fell short, stretching her arms and legs toward the far rocky wall. A fiery dragon flew up and snapped the dead woman in its gigantic ivory teeth.

It was startling for Sia to learn that even spirits could perish in this world. Still, the fear of being eaten alive showed in Sia's eyes. Her husband noticed the distress on her face. Sia took a deep breath and held back her tears.

"Sia, hold on to the end of my sash," said Xai. "When I jump, you jump."

Sia gripped the end of Xai's sash, wrapped the crimson fabric around her arm, and told herself—*live, live, live.* Xai leaned his body back and pitched his legs forward, taking a mighty leap over the extensive rocks. High in the air, Sia looked down at the monsters below. Their tongues stretched out and their hot breath reached her toes.

Thump! Xai's powerful landing shattered the rocky ground upon contact. He turned around just in time to catch Sia. She saw her own image in her husband's dark eyes, and it made her feel safe. He heard her heart pounding inside her chest, as he held her in his arms. He sensed something coming and instantly pushed Sia behind him.

Following them was a demented, odious spirit. She lifted off the ground, flying through the air, and braced herself for a close landing near Xai. The spirit was strong. Her foul, decomposing toes were nearly on the ground. With a swing of his arm, Xai created a heavy wind forceful enough to blow the deadly woman back to the valley of beasts. She fell right into the mouth of a fiery dragon.

Sia's eyes widened in amazement. She didn't question how he got his powers. She just stood dutifully behind him. One by one the spirits advanced from peak to peak, and one by one they met the forceful wind from Xai's hand that sent them into the mouths of hungry, aggressive dragons and tigers. His hands were bigger than before, stronger looking, and his nails had grown half an inch. Sia watched her husband with wide eyes. She knew he was dead, but he seemed even more different now.

How? She was puzzled. *Maybe it's a touch of both heavenly and hellish gifts.* He was definitely not the soft-spoken man she had married.

The last two spirits landed firmly on the next mountain, despite Xai's wind. One of the spirits was the one who had brought Xai back from the dead—the demon bride. Sia recognized the gold diamond-shape ring on the demon bride's hand. The other was the last spirit to have appeared among the thirteen. She appeared centuries older than the demon bride, and was withered away to bones, with only strands of white hair left on her skull. These two spirits were stronger than the rest, and they showed it by walking right through the wind that Xai had produced, standing inches from his nose, challenging him.

Xai put down his arm and turned away. Sia caught a clear view of his face; his fangs were larger. The spirits followed behind

Xai with doubtful expressions. They glared at one another, sending secret thoughts from one dead woman to another.

Did he attack us?

Yes, he attacked us.

The spirits put up their guard. Long black strands of their hair suddenly sprouted from their heads and latched onto Xai's sash. They were not going to let him roam too far anymore. The group of four continued walking. They traveled over three more mountains, above the vast valleys of dragons and tigers.

CHAPTER 5
RIVERS OF BLOOD

Xai, Sia, and the two spirits had come to a new land. This one was darker than the last, with rivers on each side of the path that ran red and were thicker than blood. The dense fog all around them created a haunting scene, hiding the reality of the red rivers as the path grew narrow.

A sweet metallic smell mixed with a smothering, pungent scent choked Sia's breath. She breathed into her sleeves. She was familiar with the smell of blood, but she could not see the rivers at that moment. The way ahead was hidden in the thick gray and white fog. Xai wasn't slowing down. Sia had to walk faster to keep up with him.

"Do you smell that?" she asked him.

"Yes," said Xai.

"Where is it coming from?"

"All around us."

She didn't know what he meant, and she could not see much around herself. She sniffed the air. The word was on the tip of her tongue, but she doubted herself. *Surely, it cannot be blood.*

"What is it?" asked Sia.

"Blood."

Sia cast her eyes around again, becoming paranoid. Even though she could not see it, now that she knew what it was, Sia became more afraid than she had been before. The two remaining spirits moved forward, with their hair still attached to Xai's sash. They floated forward past him and disappeared into the cotton-like fog, but strands of their hair were still linked to Xai.

Xai knew it was time to leave his wife. He told her, "Sia, stay here. I must go. I will return after a full thirteen days."

He's leaving? Sia felt distressed. "I can't go with you?"

He answered, "Not beyond this place." With a swift swipe of his fingers, Xai cut off the branch of a tree. The leaves were lime green, as rich in color as green grapes. He planted it in the dirt.

"If the leaves from this branch shed and wither away, and the sound of the *ncas* dies, then I will not return."

He reached inside his shirt and took out the *ncas*, hanging it on the branch. "But if this branch grows new leaves, and the *ncas* sounds off on its own, then I will return, Sia. Remember, Sia, if the leaves don't come back and the *ncas* doesn't play again, I will not return. And you must go home. Do you understand?"

Sia was scared of being left in this place, but she nodded.

"I trust you. Return to me," said Sia.

Xai wanted to touch her face, but by the time his hand reached the pure skin on her pink cheek, he saw how transformed his own hand was; he had claws like that of a wild creature. He stopped himself. She didn't mind, and reached for his large rough hand, but Xai immediately turned his back to her. For a moment, the loving couple stood in silence without words. Then Xai took a step away and distanced himself from his beautiful wife. Her eyes welled up with tears. Her mouth opened, and she wanted to call out to him, but she didn't know what to say. He didn't stop, and he didn't look back. Their hearts were breaking.

Sia watched her husband walk farther and farther away until his figure was no longer visible through the misty fog. She took a step forward, but stopped herself.

Where had Xai gone?

She dared not. Her hand clutched at her heart. *Courage.* She didn't have enough courage to defy her husband's words. She wasn't daring enough to see what lay beyond this part of the world. She knew he was protecting her. From the moment they had met, he had always protected her.

She was standing alone on a narrow path, surrounded by the dark atmosphere of the underworld. The smell of blood was still in the air.

If I stay here too long, will this be the end of me?

She was unaware of the rivers filled with lost and hungry souls that flowed on both sides of the narrow passage. Faces of the guilty. Sorrows of the broken. The confused. Fallen soldiers. Withering, mourning, suffering. Trapped.

Some time had passed. The branch had grown taller than Sia.

How much time has passed?

She was not sure. Sia took refuge underneath it for shade.

She sat at the trunk and gently leaned against the auburn bark. It often became black and freezing, the sky would turn a deep red, and the air was always foggy. Nothing was as it seemed.

Time seems not to exist in this place.

So she measured time through the growing branch.

Sia wrapped herself in an oversized leaf, as though it were a furry blanket. The branch had grown into a small tree. She waited, hoping.

Then, the leaves withered and fell off the plant. Sia picked up a dying leaf and it fell apart in her hand. *No.* This worried her. There were no new leaves growing on the tree. It soon became bare, and all the leaves were dead on the ground, including the one wrapped around her.

She waited and waited. Sia looked at her hands, her thin, and bony fingers. She knew it had been many days. She touched her own face, feeling her high cheekbones and the slender sides of her cheeks. Her appearance had changed. Her stomach felt raw, like it had been feeding on its own walls. She had eaten nothing since the snails and worms, a time she wanted to forget. She often wondered if she would die if she stayed in this place any longer.

Sia grew tired and restless. She said out loud, "Xai, you lied to me. I've waited and waited, but you have not come back to me. My heart has decided; I'm going back home to my mother."

She paced in frustration, "How could he leave me here, in a place where neither the dead nor the living can stay?" Sia turned around. *Which way is the way back?* "The way back…How will I make it back home on my own?"

The fog eventually started to lift. Sia saw a familiar path. It was small, but it was there. With the fog still rising, she could not fully see where she was going, but she began to walk back home.

Soon, she found what felt like the edge of a road. Suddenly, the fog completely lifted, revealing a narrow pathway. Sia's eyes widened as she saw the rivers of imprisoned souls. Her eyes met with one of the dead, and then more faces stared back at her. It was as though they had cast a spell on her, because she heard their tortured moaning, their aching cry, and she took a step towards one of the rivers. The poor souls were somehow luring her to them.

Sia grew aware of this, and she closed her eyes. She stepped back, stopping herself from tipping over the edge. She inched backward until she reached the center of the path, where it was safe to open her eyes again. She kept her eyes on the mossy green road. One foot in front of the other, steady.

Alone, Sia walked back the way she came. She went on, and on. *Exhausted.* She finally made it back to the brink of the giant peaks.

"Am I on the right path?" Sia wondered out loud, just as she caught the sight of a bizarrely featured creature. It was a dark bird perched on an ebony tree that was split down the middle. The tree was so dark that it appeared burnt. This creature reminded her of the bird that lived in the red oak tree back home. This bird before her, however, had green eyes that were more human than animal.

"Sia is leaving, Xai is returning," chirped the black bird.

"I'm losing my mind," Sia said out loud.

"Xai is returning, Sia is leaving," repeated the black bird.

Sia heard it clearly. She looked back over her shoulders and returned her focus to the path back home.

Sia asked the black bird, "When is Xai returning?"

"Sia is leaving, Xai is returning." The black bird sang the same line.

Is this a trick?

Sia let out a breath. She understood the words of the annoying singing bird. She turned around and paced back to the narrow path.

Sia walked until she found the familiar branch, now oversized and blooming. The ncas was hanging right over Sia's head like a fruit. The branch was growing by the second, spreading its branches further, flourishing with new green sprouts of leaves. The *ncas* sounded off, a new and harmonious tune, as if someone was playing it. *Is it the thirteenth day?* She soon found herself underneath a grand, blossoming tree, abundantly green and magnificent. She was amazed, and it was the first time she felt a sense of joy in the dark world. Then, everything turned white.

CHAPTER 6
BLUE BEAST

The sight of a soft, golden light blinded Sia. *Golden.* The light took the shape of a woman, drawing closer. Her lovely toes hovered just above the ground. Her alluring eyes came in to focus. The waves of her long white hair flowed in midair. Her youthful, glowing skin was wrapped in a pure white dress. This divine woman was a goddess.

Sia's knees felt weak. There was a little fear in her, but she couldn't look away.

"Sia, you must remain here, for this very day Xai is sure to return."

The woman's voice sounded angelic, and it quickly had a calming effect on Sia, and her initial fear faded. Sia was in awe of the goddess in her presence and almost fell to her knees but regained her balance.

"However, the yellow one, the dark one, the stripped and the red ones are all not Xai," the goddess warned Sia.

What does she mean? Sia listened carefully.

"Xai is the biggest one, the very last one. There will be someone sitting on his back, carrying a qeej. He won't be the same as you remembered. The blue one. *That one* is Xai." She gifted Sia a glorious-looking object that fit in her hand, a perfect sphere. "When Xai approaches, hold this in your hand. Do not be afraid. Stomp your feet with force. Call his name, XAI, and order him to open his mouth. Then put this inside."

Sia examined the sphere with great care and curiosity. The color and light brought warmth to her face and hands. She saw the stars and a galaxy nestled in the center, it was a thing of wonder beyond comprehension.

"Whatever falls out of his mouth, don't let the others snatch it away. You must take every piece," advised the divine being.

Sia opened her mouth to speak, but the goddess sparkled and faded away. Her voice still echoed her last words until the wind carried them away.

"But what do I do with them?" Sia asked out loud.

Soon, a large figure emerged from the misty fog. It was a yellow-striped tiger. The beast came to Sia and offered her its back. *Where had it come from?*

Sia didn't give more thought to it. She refused, shaking her head. The tiger growled at her and then went on its way. A second tiger arrived, much bigger than the first, and with a heavy white coat. The white tiger offered his back to her. Again, Sia refused. Again, the hairy beast showed its teeth to her, bitterly disappointed, and then slunk away.

Just when Sia was feeling hopeless, a third beast took shape out of the fog. It had deep blue fur, dark as the night, and blue as the depths of the sea. It was greater and stronger looking than the last two tigers. Its long white canines were dripping with saliva. This was Xai, reincarnated as a beastly creature. He walked on all four paws, his weight shaking the ground beneath him. Bewildered, Sia whispered, "The legends are true: mankind reincarnates, and humans return as creatures." She recognized the man she married within the beast that stood before her. He was ten times her size and more than double the height of their humble hut. The light was gone from his eyes, but they were still the same eyes. Xai looked unaware and possessed. There was nothing human left in him.

There was a spirit, a dead woman in an old maroon dress with black pearls and a black crown sitting on his back. She was holding Xai's *qeej*. She wore a gold, diamond-shaped ring on her left hand. Sia recognized that ring; she remembered the spirit who brought Xai from his grave. The demon bride.

They were approaching Sia on the ground. Sia stood beside the lush tree, waiting nervously, taking heavy breaths. Xai, the blue beast, pressed his giant paws into the ground, breaking the earth underneath.

Sia gathered her courage. She dashed into Xai's path, stomped her feet, and called his name.

"Xai! Open your mouth!" she commanded.

The blue beast's mouth cracked open on command. Sia quickly shoved the sphere into his mouth and closed his huge jaw with both hands. Her arms felt weak. The sphere burst inside, as his mouth cracked open wide, and white light beamed out. All thirty teeth dropped to the ground, piling like ivory treasures.

The spirit leaped from Xai's back, aiming for the pile of pearly white teeth. Sia was closer and she raced for them, stacking the sharp teeth in her arms as fast as she could. The spirit landed on the ground and reached for a tooth, but Sia snatched it from in front of her. The spirit looked around her, but the ground was empty. Sia had already collected all Xai's teeth. She hid them in her dress, tied to her waist with the sash.

The angry spirit gave Sia a deathly stare, but the blue beast interrupted them. He scooped Sia up into his mouth, but he couldn't bite her properly. Sia pushed herself out from his toothless jaw and stood in front of him, unafraid.

Sia peered into his eyes, hoping that he'd recognize her. The blue tiger was muddled. They were two determined souls, facing off in the thick fog. Sia wouldn't move out of his way and for some reason unknown to him, he wouldn't harm her either. They stood, each intensely analyzing the other.

Xai lowered his head to sniff her. Sia saw that the black stripes on his forehead were not ordinary marks, but a Hmong symbol for the word home.

There must be some small part of his former self that imprinted on his new form.

Sia reached up and firmly pressed her hand on his forehead. She felt overwhelmed with emotions: love, hope, and the fear of uncertainty. Sia pressed her forehead against the midnight-blue beast's. He remained still, receiving the affection from the tiny human before him.

The demon bride disapproved of this, and she swooped between them.

Sia stepped back, ignoring the spirit. She walked in front of Xai, then peered over her shoulder, waiting for him to follow. The giant blue tiger walked behind her.

The spirit was furious. She thought of attacking Sia, and her razor-sharp nails doubled in length. She lifted her hands, ready to cut Sia's head off. The gold ring on her left hand shimmered by her eyes. It reminded the spirit that her anger and vengeance were not toward women. She refused to leave Xai, and trailed behind him, gliding through the misty fog.

CHAPTER 7
RED ROPE

Days passed as they traveled through the underworld. Xai was still a dark blue beast. He looked to Sia. She said his name. "Xai."

Xai, in his beastly form, repeated, "Xai." Little by little, he learned to mimic her words. Xai slowly regained his memory of the human girl walking next to him. Every time he stole glances at Sia, it made him feel something inside, like the warmth of the sun. Xai had also attracted new followers: more dead women.

Sia was alert, watching herself around the new spirits.

Where have they come from? Who knew a beast would draw more lost and cursed souls?

She tried to stay close to Xai, and bumped into him, stepping on his paw. "I apologize," said Sia.

"I apologize," Xai repeated. He matched her tone.

Sia wanted to clarify with him. "*I* stepped on *you*."

"*I* stepped on *you*."

"You sound like the black bird now," said Sia.

Xai repeated her, "You sound like the black bird."

"No." Sia stopped him.

"No," he copied her.

Sia asked him, "Is this your way of learning how to talk again?"

He nodded, and it surprised her.

"Say something," said Sia.

He opened his mouth, and breathed heavily, trying to speak. Nothing came out.

"Do you know who you are?" asked Sia.

He nodded.

"You're saying *yes*?"

He nodded again.

"Do you know who I am?"

He struggled to answer, but then he said with a low growl, "Yes." That made Sia smile.

"Do you know where we're going?" asked Sia.

"Yes," said Xai. His speech was better this time.

"Will you take me home?"

"Yes."

"You will?" Sia sounded hopeful.

"I will." He had a monstrous voice, but he spoke clearly.

Going through the mouths of dragons and tigers was easier than the first time. Sia sat on Xai's head and held tightly to his blue fur, while he jumped from peak to peak. The spirits cleared the rocky mountains effortlessly.

They soon reached two paths. One path led to what appeared to be the living world; it was a long, winding trail through a forest that stopped at a reflective portal, at the very end of the woods. The other path was a straight road to black mountains, which were far away. Other creatures could be seen miles away, taking the path to the black mountains.

Somewhere along the way Xai had regained his speech, and he instructed the spirits, "All of you, go ahead to the black mountains and wait for me. I'll send off my younger sister to my mother and father. Once I've returned, we can continue."

The spirits agreed and headed their separate way toward the black mountains. Onward, Xai and Sia stayed on their course. The portal could be seen, but they had been walking for days. There were no impossible trials and gigantic monsters on this path. Sia rubbed her tired legs, and Xai nudged her forward. The fog finally lifted. Sia felt the warm sunlight on her skin.

They arrived at the portal, where Sia saw their reflection. She held onto Xai's fur as they both stepped through the portal. Their sight was blinded by bright lights, then the young couple reached a place that resembled the living earth. There were green mountains beyond the forest. Familiar birds and insects fluttered in the air. The air smelled of fresh rain, pine, and wet moss. Sia took a deep breath. This was the world she remembered, and she was glad to return home at last.

The red oak tree was visible far ahead on the path. Sia's face lit up. It was the edge of their village.

The trees were blooming with pink and white flowers. It gave Sia an idea of how long they had been gone. It must have been weeks since Xai's funeral. She looked at his face and realized that Xai didn't recognize his own village.

He doesn't know we're home. Will he leave me, once he knows?

Sia stopped underneath a tree and ran in front of Xai to block his path.

"Xai, I'm starving. You wait here." Sia didn't want him to know where they were, so she made up a lie: "I will ask the Chinese couple that lives up ahead for some food. And then we can leave. Yes?"

"Yes," Xai agreed. He could see that the woman in front of him was skin and bones. Sia hurried into the nearest house. She met Xai's parents at their door, and spoke quickly, "Mother, father, I've brought Xai here. If you two hear me whistling, come out and help me." She was short of breath.

Xai's parents were confused.

"He's really here!" said Sia. "You'll know it when you hear his voice."

His parents were suddenly filled with hope and dropped everything they were doing. Together the old couple excitedly agreed, "Yes!"

Xai's father gathered a bundle of twisted brown rope, while Sia took the food covered on the table and ran out of the front door.

Xai's mother didn't bother to ask questions, instead, she went to a wooden chest.

"Red rope," said Xai's mother, as she pulled a bundle of red, braided rope from the chest.

"That's for spirits," said Xai's father.

"We buried our son," Xai's mother reminded him.

Minutes later, Sia returned to Xai. She presented him with banana leaves topped with sticky rice and deep-fried pork belly. They ate underneath the shade of a large tree, which was shedding pink petals.

"Xai, you're going your way, and I'm going mine," she said. "We may never be together again. My head is itchy. What if it's lice and there's no one to help me after you're gone? Search through my hair and I'll search through yours for the last time."

"Yes, I can do that," replied Xai.

"You look at mine first," Sia took a seat in front of the blue beast.

Xai was careful, thoroughly checking every strand of hair on her round little head. This brought cheer to him, and for a moment he felt like he belonged here. Then he noticed the great difference between them. They looked nothing alike anymore. It made him wonder why he had paws, and blue fur compared to her fair earthy skin.

They switched places. Sia stood on her toes while the blue beast laid as low as possible. Sia pretended to pick through his long dark fur, grouping strands together and tying them to the tree behind them.

Suspicion rose in Xai's mind. "How come it feels like you're tying my hair?"

"It's all knotted and tangled. I'm just combing through it." Sia kept tying his hair to the trunk of the tree. "Xai, I will be lonely. You're going your own way, and I'm going mine. Let us whistle."

"Whistle? Whistle how?" asked Xai.

"Whistle saying, Xai is going Xai's way, and Sia is going Sia's way. It's so lonely!" She wanted to trick him into speaking loudly, so that his parents could hear his voice.

Xai whistled at first, but it soon turned into words. "Xai is going Xai's way, and Sia is going Sia's way. It's so lonely."

Then it was Sia's turn. She whistled loudly and said, "Mother, Father, bring rope here!"

These words startled Xai. He asked, "Why did you whistle, 'Mother, Father, bring rope here'?"

"No, you didn't hear it right," lied Sia. "I whistled, Xai is going Xai's way, and Sia is going Sia's way. It's so lonely."

Two old people raced towards Sia and the blue beast, with bundles of thick red rope in their hands. Confused, Xai leaped to his feet. He was forcefully yanked backwards by his tied fur. *Thump!* Xai released a beastly cry, toothless and afraid.

"Xai, you're a man," said Sia. "Why would you cry like that?"

That baffled Xai for a second. "How should I cry then?"

She instructed, "Cry out, Mother and Father!"

Xai growled, "Mother! Father!"

"You didn't cry like a real man. You still sound like an animal."

Xai was just about to try again, but the old couple jumped onto his furry body. Xai's large tiger head was pressed to the ground. Xai looked at the old man and woman tying him up with red rope, and his eyes widened as he recognized them as his mother and father. He felt his strength drain from his body. He clawed at the red rope, and the claws broke off against the red fibers. The red rope made him weak.

As the old couple secured the knots over Xai's hairy form, they looked at each other with confused faces. *This is a beast. Where is our son?* The giant tiger under them pushed up, and they forced it back down.

"Sia?" Xai felt betrayed, and it echoed from his voice.

The old couple double knotted the rope, then they cut him loose from the tree. The fear and confusion from Xai's eyes as he was dragged away by his own parents broke Sia a little inside.

"Let me go! I cannot stay here!" shouted Xai. He tried calling to her again, "Sia."

She was too ashamed to return Xai's gaze. She kept her eyes to the ground and followed behind them. She had tricked him because she loved him. She kept her mouth shut.

"Sia!" His cry swelled into the air and unleashed a loud roar that scared off all the small creatures nearby. Even the white horse, Dawb, was startled.

CHAPTER 8
COW MANURE

Xai's eyes opened. His dark blue body was deep in a thick, and heavy pool of mud. He was in a hole deep in the ground, just outside a little fenced-in hut.

The smell was terrible. Xai realized he was soaking chest deep in animal feces. Cow manure. He cringed, and struggled to move, but he was powerless.

Xai looked up and recognized the human faces watching him. Sia and Xai's parents sat around the edge of the manmade poop pond, discussing the situation. Tools and supplies were scattered around them messily.

"Are you certain this is our son?" Xai's mother asked.

"Yes," replied Sia. "Without a doubt."

"He's a tiger…and our son is dead."

"There are sayings that claim our people can die and become beasts," said Xai's father. "We cannot disregard the message and warnings in old tales just because they are stories."

"If this is our son, then we must help him." Xai's mother glanced at him in the reeking pond. "Cow manure is known to work against spirits and strange creatures."

"There's nothing more we can do." Xai's father gathered his tools. "I must share the news with the villagers. They're already gathering and talking."

Spirits of the dead gathered in the area, lurking near the forest and then hiding in the shadows around the building. The spirits were drawn to Xai, but they couldn't identify the creature covered in cow manure. Xai could see the spirits, but he didn't know what they were anymore, or why they were there watching him. The demon bride had arrived. Her burgundy dress swayed, as did her long, thick hair, as she attempted to sniff Xai out.

Day in and day out, Sia committed to being by Xai's side. Villagers and relatives came by to check on Sia and the beast they had heard about, hoping it was truly Xai. Then one evening Xai had an awakening; he knew something was different.

"Sia, boil some water. Please. I'd like to take a bath and eat," Xai proclaimed in a tired tone. It was the first human thing he had said in a long time.

"I'll boil some water," Sia said gladly.

She tried to help Xai get out of the cow manure pond. It took a few more people to successfully pull him out onto dry land. Sia started a fire and poured water into a large pot.

The sudden noise of birds startled her. Sia went to the back of the house, following some disturbing slurping sounds. She caught Xai devouring raw chicken eggs. Broken shells were caught in his sharp teeth, and golden yolks oozed from his bottom lip.

Sia was shocked to see that he had new baby fangs. *He's not human yet.* She screamed at the top of her lungs, "Help!"

Immediately, Xai burst out of the henhouse. He was soon completely surrounded by his parents and a group of villagers armed with machetes, arrows, and knives long enough to be swords. The villagers captured him with hardly any trouble. His parents tied him up again with the red rope, and Sia pushed his massive body back into the pond of foul cow manure.

"We're helping you," said Sia.

Xai grunted and jerked around, and then more cow manure washed over him. The stinky material just kept piling up around Xai. He was in head deep, leaving only his nose free to breathe, his eyes to see, and his ears to hear. Xai stopped fighting. He surrendered. The giant cat soaked in black goo like a stone statue, with flies zooming about his head.

Xai glanced at Sia, seeing her kind expression. It grew quiet between the two of them. She watched him faithfully, without care for the uncomfortable environment or the damage to her lovely handmade dress. Her eyes grew tired, but she refused to leave the sight of him.

Days elapsed. Sia sang to Xai when the moon was full and close to the earth. She endured the long days and cold nights on the dirty ground. The strong smell of cow manure faded as they both grew used to it. There were moments when Sia would look at Xai and see his gaze becoming more human. She combed her fingers through the fur on his crown, and hummed a soft tune. Alive, dead, or beast, he was still her husband.

One day, Dawb, the white horse, trotted over to Sia and sat next to her. Sia told the horse, "I'm glad that you're not afraid anymore, Dawb."

Finally, Xai broke his silence. His voice was low and weak, but it had a man's voice.

"Sia…" He struggled to speak. "I can't bear it anymore. I can no longer stay here. Please, pull me out. Take my hand."

Sia nodded. She reached into the pool of cow manure and searched for Xai's hand. She touched what felt like fingers instead of paws. Excited, Sia took hold and pulled him out. Xai had shed his blue fur. His fair skin had returned. All ten fingers and all ten toes. His hair had turned jet black again. Xai's face was once more human. He was beautiful. A gasp of joy mixed with astonishment escaped Sia's lips. She slid her fingers between his. They fit like they used to. She rejoiced and embraced him.

Sia poured a second round of hot water into a tub made of clay. Xai settled in the clay tub, and the steam rose from the surface of the water, relaxing him. Sia ran her fingers through Xai's fine hair. So lovely and perfect.

She left him to wash himself, and she washed her hair with warm water in the clay tub in front of her. The scent of rose petals rose with the steam and relaxed her from a weary string of events. She kept an eye on him as she cleaned herself, wiping her face with a wet cloth. She dried her hair and wore it down, with floral arrangements pinned to one side.

She stepped into the bamboo shed behind the clay tub to put on a new dress the color of peach blossoms. Beside her was a large, long wooden box containing her red dress and the collection of tiger teeth that she had saved from the netherworld. She closed the box and covered it with a red sheet. She pushed the box back, and it scraped the floor. Sia looked to Xai; he was still soaking in the hot clay tub. The noise hadn't seemed to bother him.

She returned to apply more force to the box, and it finally slid down a bamboo ramp that led into the lower level of the shed.

Oink. Oink. Little piglets were watching her from the backdoor.

"Back outside." Sia chased the brown and pink piglets out. She secured the closed door with a stone. She could hear the little pigs oinking among themselves from behind the backdoor.

Later that evening, they both sat at the dining table. Sia placed a bowl of rice noodle porridge in front of Xai. He leaned in and slurped the porridge, making up for days of fasting. He ate the boiled chicken, steamed vegetables, pickled mustard greens, fried eggs, and rice. Xai seemed to have gained back his strength. His cheeks flushed pink, and his lips were peachy.

Sia watched him eat, cherishing this simple moment. Xai raised his head, met his wife's eyes, and he smiled at her. She smiled back, and began to eat.

Late that night, while the two lay in bed, Sia combed her fingers through his hair. She felt grateful; she hadn't thought she could be so fortunate.

"I was dead, and you brought me back. Why?" Xai asked, earnestly.

The thought of living without him broke Sia's heart again. "I was completely empty without you."

Xai looked to his wife. "Forgive me. I promised you a full life together. One hundred and twenty years." He brushed the hair at her cheek. "And then I left you so soon, and in a place with strangers. Things must have been difficult for you."

"They were," Sia said. "Some of your relatives planned to marry me off to a blind man."

"How awful. Did you decline their offer?"

"I would have *strongly* declined their offer, but I was afraid to embarrass your family. I didn't say a word."

"You didn't have to abandon who you truly are to marry me. You've always been strong-willed, with a strong mind."

"I am, and I followed you into the dark world."

"Why did you do that?"

"Why did you make such a request?" asked Sia. "Water to wash your face and food to feast on after the third day of your funeral?"

"As Hmong, it's tradition. The living family members must feed their dead three days after the burial and continue to invite them to eat every meal for a complete year after until the day their soul is set free."

"The release of the spirit," said Sia.

"Yes."

She admitted, "I know very little of Hmong funeral and burial traditions."

"Well, one year after the burial, the dead must have their spirit released to be free in order to live in the afterlife or be reincarnated."

"But you rose from the dead."

"I did." Xai felt blessed. "And you followed me into death and brought me back to life. I am a fortunate man to have such a brave and beautiful wife."

He held her close and took in the scent of her hair. His lips parted from the floral aroma. It was euphoric. They laid in each other's arms in the bed that was theirs. The yellow glow from the candlelight bounced off their creamy skin. All was quiet, calm.

Sia felt whole again. She exhaled, content. "Tell me a story."

"You've heard them all." Xai sounded tired. He closed his eyes.

"I like hearing you tell old tales." She spoke softly. "It is as if I am there."

"Tell me a story from your people," said Xai.

"The stories from my people are mostly cautionary tales."

"Tell me your favorite one."

"Beware of spirits, for they come in the form of man and animals."

"Spirits of the dead?" asked Xai. "They're shapeshifters?"

"Yes…" Sia thought for a moment. "Maybe something older. Demons."

"Demons."

The image of the demon bride crossed Sia's mind.

"Has anyone from your village ever seen one?" asked Xai.

"Yes," Sia recalled, "My father. Men and children from the village talked about an old woman who tormented them in the night while they slept. They called her the *old hag*. Villagers were dying in their sleep. One night, my father woke up to see an old woman standing in at his feet. He always kept a silver knife under his pillow. He grabbed the knife and swung at her, just as she leaped onto his body. The old woman lost a hand before she escaped through the window. My father chased her across the roofs of the village homes, but she was too fast for him, and then she vanished into the woods. He wanted evidence, so he returned to his room to look for the hand of the old woman, but found the paw of a cat in its place."

"That is a terrifying story. Did the old woman ever return?"

"No, at least not to our village. The old woman has become a cautionary tale."

"It seems that not all stories are only cautionary tales. I believe that now."

Sia glanced at him. "Perhaps someday, people will tell our story. Not as a cautionary tale, but as a love story. Stories are all we will become in the end. I want us to be remembered as two people who loved each other."

Those words made Xai smile. He replied, "It is comforting to know we'll be remembered."

"Yes, it is."

Xai rubbed his wife's shoulder and softly said, "Sleep now, wife."

"Tell me a story," said Sia. "I can't fall asleep."

"Why not?"

"What if I wake up tomorrow and you're not really here?" She said, fearfully. "And this has all been a dream."

"Which one, then?" asked Xai. He recalled the list of stories that he knew. "The witch who devours human heads? A story of dragons? Or the Mao-Hlub?"

"Why do people call it the Mao-Hlub? It's a strange name for a very large beast." Sia had so many questions. "How do people know what it looks like? If the Mao-Hlub ate humans, who lived to tell such a tale?"

"They say the Mao-Hlub is a giant creature with the body of a man. It's as hairy as a bear, and it has a very large mouth. It will grab your arm and laugh at the sky." Xai's deep, dark tone inspired fear. "If the sky is sunny and bright, then it will let you go, but if the sky grows dark and gray, then it will eat you!"

Sia's face lit up with excitement.

"The creature has no kneecaps or elbows, so if it falls, it will struggle to get up. Now, heed the warning. Wear bamboo sleeves on your arms, so that if you ever encounter a Mao-Hlub and it grabs you by the arm, you can slip away quickly and run while it loses its balance. Can you image the giant creature wobbling on the ground?"

Sia chuckled at the thought. "Are there witnesses? How do people know that such a creature exists?"

"They just do. There's a creature even bigger and scarier than a Mao-Hlub. Creatures of all kinds exist." Xai looked her in the eyes. "You believe in the old hag. Spirits. Demons. You have traveled into the world of the dead and have seen things no other human has."

They looked at each other. He was right, and Sia knew it. She felt troubled by something. She didn't quite know what it was yet, but she was worried for them. He saw the concern on her face.

"What is it, wife?" asked Xai.

The demon bride crossed her mind again. *Why?*

"I'm not sure," said Sia. "Maybe it's nothing."

She placed her head on his chest. The sound of his steady heartbeat made her calm.

"Do you remember the day we met?" Sia asked.

It took Xai a moment to recall. "I do. You had no shoes, and I thought you were a man because you were dressed like one."

They both chuckled at the memory.

"When did you first start liking me?" asked Sia.

"You know the answer."

"Yes, but I'd like to hear it again."

Xai lifted her chin up to look at him. "The moment I knew you were a woman."

"And why did you like me?"

"It was difficult not to fall for you. You're honest. You're brave. Even in the face of death, you didn't give up. You're naive, yet more educated and capable than me. You thought that being a woman was your flaw, but you are the strongest person I've ever met."

"You have not met a lot of people," Sia chuckled.

Xai laughed with her, and held her closer. "I don't need to. There's no one else for me...I've missed you."

Sia released a sigh of relief. "I've missed you, too."

As Xai lay silently in deep thought, something bothered him. "Sia, there's something you must do. Fasten a device, a long pole to stir the pond of manure. Whatever you find, you must fish it out and get rid of it."

That sounded easy enough, but Sia recognized the look on his face and knew that he had more to say. She stayed silent, listening intently.

"The fur cannot stay, it will eventually try to become one with me again." He explained, trying not to frighten her. "You must take it far, far away. Climb the highest mountain and cast it away on the other side." Xai sounded more serious than he had ever been before, like he had aged ten years. "Before you cast it away, you must also speak these words, *'If you all want your old possessions, come and claim them'*. Then, you, Sia, must throw it away immediately and run. Do not look back."

"How do you know what must be done?"

"Through death and the underworld, knowing is something imprinted on me. Like a cautionary tale that lives deep in my bones."

She thought about the collection of tiger teeth that she had hidden earlier. "Just the fur, then. Nothing else needs to be returned?"

"Yes, just the fur."

"Why can't you go with me?"

"I cannot go to the ends of the earth with the fur, for I am still part of their world, and they will rightfully take me."

Sia was deeply troubled. *It's not over.*

CHAPTER 9
THE FUR

S
ia went past the pigs and entered the shed through the backdoor. She pulled out the large wooden box wrapped with red cloth from beneath the shed. She opened the top to reveal the pile of long, sharp white teeth.

While Xai slept soundly in bed, Sia sat in the corner of the house inventing a new gadget: a long ivory pole with a hook at the end. She tied the two ends of the pole together with rope while stealing glances at Xai. He was in a calm, deep slumber. Finally, when she had finished the device, Sia was ready to fish out the fur from the smelly pond. She held her invention back at arm's length, and admired the new tool. It looked more like a weapon, an ivory pole with an iron tip. Much like an iron sickle.

The strange feeling that she associated with supernatural forces returned. Sia felt shadows creeping around the outside of the house. The hair on her arms stood up.

"Go away. You're not welcome here," whispered Sia, trying to be brave. She could see her breath escape her lips. It had suddenly grown cold inside the house.

She glanced at her husband. The candlelight in the corner burned bright yellow. He was tucked nicely under the thickly woven blanket.

Suddenly, the candle next to her blew out on its own. She gasped from fright.

"The broom. Where is the broom?" Sia spoke out loud to herself.

She set the wooden pole tool down by the wall and searched the kitchen in the dark. Her hand found the broomstick; she instantly recognized it from sweeping the house so often. She hurried to the front door and hung the broom beside it.

"How did father say it?" said Sia, trying to remember what he used to say. "Broom, watch our home." She paused, and thought hard. Then she changed her tone to a more confident and strong voice. "Broom, stay here by the door. Watch our home well. You see all things at this door. Do not allow anything or anyone inside that will do us harm. Keep evil spirits out." She patted the broom to make sure it stayed still.

Sia tiptoed over to her husband and climbed into bed. She wrapped her arms around him and held him close. He felt her warm body next to his, and her breath was near his face.

"Were you talking to the broom?" asked Xai, with a soft voice.

"Yes," said Sia.

"Why?

"My father used to do it."

"What for?"

"To keep evil spirits out."

Xai placed an arm over her. "You're safe," he told her. "Sleep, wife."

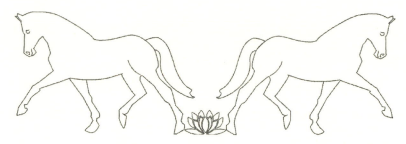

Before the sun had risen, Sia was already standing at the rim of the manure pond. She faced the task, as if she was facing a dragon. Strong. Determined.

Sia rolled up her sleeves and got to work, inserting the new ivory pole with the iron sickle into the manure. She gagged. The white horse neighed at her, in a teasing way.

Sia stepped back and hid her face in the sleeve of her arm, ducking from the unpleasant smell. This wasn't working. The sunrise cast a warm light in front of her. Suddenly, she had an idea. She took out the pole and set it to the side.

Moments later she returned with her face half covered with layers of fabric that pulled over her mouth and nose like a mask. That definitely helped with the foul-smelling work. Sia placed the long device back into the cow manure and continued to stir it around and around. She pushed the pole further, almost dipping her hands in the disgusting muck. She shouted in fright, and she pulled her hands back a little. Chickens clucked as they passed by, almost as though they were laughing at her. Dawb, the white horse, let out a short neigh, definitely laughing at her.

Then, Sia's arms felt the weight of something heavy. The iron sickle had caught something. She attempted to pull it out, battling with it for a moment. It was like a fish trying to get away. Sia pulled and pulled, taking one step back at a time. The sun was high in the sky now, and brought heat down on the crown of her head. Small slivers of steam rose from the manmade pond. Sia gagged and turned her head to the side, coughing.

The orange sunset created red colors in the horizon behind Sia. The pole was almost completely out of the manure pond. She reached forwards, one hand in front of the other, getting feces in her fingernails. The tip of the iron sickle broke the surface and brought along with it the deep blue and black fur. The skin of a tiger emerged like a monster.

Sia's heart pounded loudly in her chest as she grasped the fur coat, pulling it further and further out. She let go of the silver tool, took hold of the skin with both hands, and yanked the fur coat completely out of the disgusting pond. The heavy dark blue fur skin plopped out and landed on Sia like a blanket. She found herself unable to move underneath such a massive amount of skin and fur, especially as it was covered in cow manure. There was dung in her hair, and she was covered in feces. Disgusted, Sia wriggled, but she was helpless. She was stuck for the time being. All she could do now was take deep breaths. It made the fur seem as if it were alive once more. Her face turned sour at the horrible smell. She shut her eyes to calm herself and try to forget the stench, and the poop, and the day's strange event.

The wind brushed over Sia, and through the fur coat. Whispers of a strange language came with the breeze. Sia opened her eyes wide, and she laid still, listening. She recognized the ancient words.

Worry overwhelmed her. Sia pushed and crawled onto her back. Finally, she was able to force herself out from underneath the heavy beastly skin. She pulled off the layers of fabric from her face, and glanced around her surroundings cautiously. She looked behind her. The sun had disappeared over the mountains. Sia faced the deep green peaks. The silhouette of higher mountains rested beyond those familiar peaks. The highest point of the giant rocks seemed to disappear into the sky. That was the next place she must journey to.

Hot steam rose from a clay tub that sat on a raised silver bed. Dying firewood glowed red and pink beneath it. Buckets of muddy water and dirty clothes sat to the side. Pigs and chickens were still awake in their closed quarters, but the noise of the animals faded in the background. She was clean now, and sank into the water for a moment of bliss as the firewood underneath the tub became ashes.

Her eyes caught the sight of her wrinkling fingers, and in plain sight was the box of ivory teeth that laid a yard away. *It was time to work again.*

CHAPTER 10
NEW JOURNEY

The next morning, Sia harnessed the rolled-up fur to a wagon behind the white horse. She slipped on an ivory bow and fastened silver arrows into a leather case. She hid a silver knife securely in the sash of her dress. "Dawb," she said to the horse. "I need your help." She gently brushed Dawb's ivory mane. "I have to travel into the mountains. Will you come with me?"

The white horse nodded. This brought a smile to Sia's pale face and lit her up with hope. Footsteps suddenly sounded at the front door. It was Xai.

Sia met her husband in front of their home. She wrapped her arms around him and held him close for a moment. She took a good look at him, adoring him. Xai seemed to be recovering well, except for the dark circles underneath his eyes and the weak appearance of his posture. "You hardly slept," he said. He touched the bone of the bow. "What is this made out of?"

"The teeth of a supernatural beast," Sia said. "I was told to take them. I'm sure I can keep them."

Xai recognized the ivory material. "I see." He returned to the more pressing matter. "I apologize for not being able to make the journey with you."

Sia nodded in acceptance. "I'm not disappointed, husband." It was enough that he was here talking to her. She would do anything in her power to keep them together, but for now, she tied a red string around his wrist and whispered words of protection over him. They didn't know how to say goodbye, for in their language there is no such word.

"Hurry back to me," said Xai.

"I shall try." Then Sia released his hand and departed.

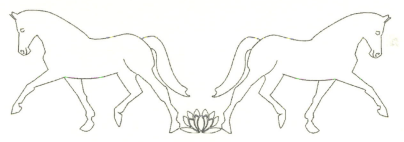

Sia went on her way, pulling the white horse past the wooden gate of their home. They headed toward the highest peak, which was a place they had never journeyed to. Xai stood at the doorway, watching them until they disappeared over the horizon.

After hours of traveling, the day gave way to the night. The scent of white pine mixed with sweet maple leaves filled the air. Silence. Not a single bird or creature lurked about. The woods grew thicker and the trail narrower. Soon there was something different in the air, a musky smell and an unnatural haze which grew thicker by the second. The branches were creaking and rubbing together, as a strong breeze combed through them and spooked the horse.

"It's just the wind." Sia attempted to calm the horse, brushing his white mane.

The trees in front of them shifted. The rustling of unknown creatures and shadows moving around them nearly caused the horse to turn back.

"Don't be afraid." Sia spoke to the horse, "We have to keep going and find a safe place to sleep."

Again, the trees on both sides of the path moved. The forest was playing tricks on them. Dawb panicked and picked up his pace, galloping down the narrow road.

The trees began to slide into their path. Sia helped the horse swerve around a tree. Her shoulder scraped the bark, and a branch took a slice of skin at her neck, drawing blood. They rode through the mysteriously wicked forest for what seemed like hours.

Dawb was tired, and he stopped walking.

Sia said to the horse, "We can't turn back yet." She closed her eyes. "Something is doing this," said Sia, trying to make sense of the enchanted forest. She opened her eyes. "Please let us through!" Sia shouted around her. It made the horse a little uneasy, and he trotted back. Sia stabilized him. "We mean no harm!" Sia shouted to the trees. "We are just passing through! Please!"

Then, there was suddenly a path that opened up in front of them. "This way," said Sia, patting Dawb on the side. She directed him down the new path. She looked to the trees and shouted, "Thank you!"

The forest thinned out. Fewer and fewer trees were in sight. It was dark ahead, although it was only midday. What lay ahead shocked the two travelers. It was a large, steep mountain. The way up was flat like a stone wall, and there was no path visible.

"How do we get around this mountain?" Sia mused out loud. Her eyes followed the mighty black rock upward as it rose to the sky. It seemed to disappear into the fluffy gray clouds. "It reaches the heavens. How have we not seen this mountain from the village?" She dragged the horse along the side of the black rock, which seemed to keep growing larger by the minute. "This way, Dawb. We must find a way around this mountain."

As the sun came out from the clouds, light beamed onto the side of the black mountain, showing Sia the way. There was a large opening into the rocky mountain, a cave. Sia got off the horse. She stood at the mouth of the cave. Suddenly, a gust of wind pushed her backward. Her back hit the nose of the horse.

Sia turned to the horse, and said, "We can't climb this mountain, so we must go through it." Dawb stomped his hooves, disagreeing with her.

"Are you afraid of the cave?" asked Sia. Dawb made a whinnying sound.

She glanced back at the way they had come. The forest appeared less threatening now. "You don't have to come with me if you're scared. You know the way home."

The horse nudged her onward with his nose, which put a slight smile on her face. She pressed her forehead to his. Deep down, she felt that something bigger lay ahead, and she shook with nerves.

"I'm scared, too," said Sia, softly. She was not ready, but she was not alone, and grateful for that.

Sia went back to the horse's side, digging into a bag. She pulled out some supplies and lit a wick for her oil lamp. Then she took the reins and led the horse into the mouth of the cave. The lamp illuminated the space around them, lighting the way. Together, Sia and the white horse entered the darkness, into the mouth of the cave. Sia realized she had experienced this sort of situation before. She was now entering another unfathomable world.

CHAPTER 11
CURSED

The path inside the cave was dark at first, but Sia's eyes soon adjusted. She and the horse could only see as far as the light could reach, no more than a few feet around them. She breathed in stale air, and her face turned sour at the strange musk. The walls of the cave shone. White crystals that twinkled like stars were fused with the stonewalls.

Sia tilted her head up. The ceiling of the cave stretched high above, embedded with glowing drops of light. Sia realized that they were glow-worms. The cave no longer seemed quite as dark; it was almost magical.

The sound of water dripping and running echoed from different parts of the cave. The uneven ground was layered with moss. They passed by a carcass of a half-eaten deer. Sia realized that must have been the strange smell from earlier, but it was worse now that they were at the source. She covered her nose and pressed on.

The smell in the cave grew more foul by the minute. Sia covered her nose and mouth with her sleeve. The stench was so strong, it made her cough. They passed another animal carcass. Sia hung the lantern on a rope tied to the horse's side, so she could lead the horse with one hand and cover her own face properly to escape the unpleasant smell.

"It's another dead animal. Don't be spooked, Dawb," said Sia, as she stroked the horse's side to calm him down.

They kept walking, the smell getting stronger still, but now there were no remains of any kind of animal in sight. Sia glanced behind her. There was a figure far behind them that resembled an old woman. Sia blinked, and the figure disappeared.

Sia suddenly felt tired. Her eyes grew heavy. She pulled the white horse back, slowed down, and said, "Let's rest here. We've traveled day and night. How ambitious of us, and foolish," she said. She leaned up against a rock wall and sat down. Something about this place made her feel unsafe. She was sleepy, but fought it for as long as she could, which only lasted minutes. She closed her eyes for just a moment and fell asleep while sitting with her back against a rock wall.

Sia suddenly opened her eyes. She could see the white horse out of the corner of her eyes, but something was not right.

Sia couldn't turn her head. She looked down at her feet. There was the old woman again. The old hag was on all fours, low to the ground like a deadly predator, grinning from ear to ear. Sia's heart hammered in her chest. She was frozen with fear, unable to move.

The old hag grabbed Sia by the ankles. Her long thin fingers spidered up Sia's legs. The old hag opened her mouth, and unleashed a long black tongue, licking the dirt on Sia's right shin. Sia panicked, but her lips remained tightly shut. She glared at her horse, but Dawb seemed to be asleep.

The hag was now sitting on top of Sia, holding her shoulders down. Her wrinkled feet pressed on Sia's thighs, which felt like a thousand pounds of pressure on Sia. The old hag's pointy nose was only an inch away from poking Sia's.

Sia struggled on the inside, but she was stiff as a stick. She wanted to scream, but she still couldn't make a sound.

The hag stretched her mouth open, tearing her lips at the sides clear across her rotten cheeks, and leaned closer, as if to feast on Sia's head. She tightened her grip on Sia and yanked Sia's shoulders upward. Time slowed down. Everything was happening in slow motion. Sia felt her own body lifting off the ground. Tiny black pebbles levitated into the air.

Sia looked down. She could see her body lying still on the ground, although she was also floating in the air. Sia suddenly realized that she must be dreaming. The horse appeared to be sleeping, so she must be too. But the old, horrific hag was taking her. Her heart seemed to be racing at a thousand beats per minute, and she was afraid it would stop beating and then she would die. *Is this how people die in their dreams?*

TUG! The old hag couldn't move up any higher. *Tug. Tug.* The hag glanced down at Sia's body, and Sia did the same. Sia's silver necklace, the spirit lock, was anchoring her soul to her physical body. The hag yanked on Sia's soul, but she struggled to pull it any further.

Sia clenched her jaw down so hard that blood ran down the sides of her mouth. She let out a roar, shouting at the old hag. She had bitten her own tongue trying to wake herself up, and it had worked. She jolted awake, shouting.

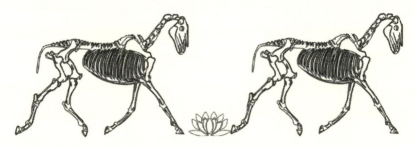

The old hag was nowhere in sight. The horse stood up, startled by Sia's wailing. Sia realized she spooked Dawb. She went to the horse, calming him down with a soft touch. "Shhh," she said, softly.

Sia looked around quickly, feeling eyes watching her, and a chill went down her spine. Curious and cautious, Sia looked over her shoulder. There was a figure behind them, low to the ground, and it hadn't been there before. Sia squinted. The figure stood up, lifting its head. An old woman with long, frizzy hair, who was missing a hand, looked back at them. It was the same vile hag from Sia's dream.

Sia's eyes doubled in size. She pulled the horse forward and ran. The fear pounded loudly in her chest. The old hag was real.

Whoosh! Suddenly, the hag materialized right in front of Sia, flying at her with razor-sharp teeth. Her long nails swung at the horse's reins. Sia pushed the horse forward, shouting, "Run, Dawb!"

The horse took off, galloping forward. The old hag's mouth missed Sia's cheek, but her long nails cut clear across the reins, ropes, and bags on the horse, and then she headed straight for Sia's neck. Sia dodged the attack and fell behind a boulder. She rolled over quickly and quietly.

Loud hoofbeats echoed against the rocky walls as the horse charged along the open path through the cave. *Clink. Clank.* A racket sounded behind the horse as it bolted away. Food supplies and blankets fell off the horse as he got further and further away from Sia.

Sia was relieved the horse had gotten away. She flinched at the pain in her left shoulder. The fabric was shredded, and she was bleeding. The old hag hadn't missed her completely.

Standing in front of her, the old hag wiped Sia's blood onto her black tongue. "I know your ancestors."

Sia slowly raised her head to see the old hag savoring the blood from her long black fingers to the ugly spiky nails. Disgusted, Sia's brows crinkled inward. She saw again that the old hag only had one hand. Sia wiped the blood from her shoulder onto the side of the rock. "You're missing a hand," Sia yelled at the hag. Her voice echoed through the cave. The old hag rushed to her location, but Sia was already gone. She was hidden elsewhere.

"You are just a girl. Naïve. Weak. Human." The old hag licked her fingers clean. "Flesh."

Sia gathered a handful of black pebbles, and then threw them into the air. The rocks scattered everywhere. Sia rushed to another large rock wall and shouted, "I know you!"

"As I know you," said the old hag. She was getting the scent of Sia from several places. It confused her nose.

"Why did you try to kill my father? He has never offended anyone." Sia smeared her blood on the rock and moved on to her next hiding place. She rolled into a crack beneath the next boulder.

The old hag swept past. Her bony toes were inches from Sia's face. "His bloodline allows me to take him," said the hag, as she found Sia's blood smeared on the side of the rock. It angered the old hag to be tricked, "Blood of his blood." She fled from the rock, and looked elsewhere.

Sia searched the ground for rocks bigger than her own fists, and found two. "Why?" She tossed the rocks in the opposite direction and ran again.

"The reason is older than I. Older than those who came before me."

Sia found a large rock. She held it at her waist. The rock banged against something solid. Sia looked down at her sash and saw the small bamboo case hanging at her side. "There are others like you?"

The old hag realized where Sia was hiding, and smiled wickedly. "We are many." Many voices came from the old hag's mouth. She stepped into the shadows and vanished.

Sia, now terrified by the voices of the hag, pulled out a small hunting knife from the bamboo case. She gathered her courage and asked, "Are my people cursed?"

The sharp teeth gleamed behind the old hag's black grin. "Just the men."

Sia flung the rock into the darkness, hoping to divert the old hag once again. It worked. The hag scurried toward the fallen stone. Sia stood up and came out from behind the boulder, grasping tightly to the knife.

Suddenly, the old hag appeared right in front of Sia. "Occasionally, a woman." She raked her sharp nails at Sia's face, aiming for her eyes.

Sia quickly swung the knife. The old hag's fingers cut a few strands of Sia's hair, but Sia sliced off her hand. Dark black blood spilled from the hag's arm. The old hag let out an agonizing shriek that echoed from the walls of the cave. Sia watched the hag's hand hit the ground, and it transformed to the paw of a large cat. Sia didn't stop to get a better look. She dashed off after the horse. The old hag screamed after her, reaching out both her arms, handless and bleeding after Sia.

Startled, Sia gasped, running as fast as her short legs could carry her. She nearly stumbled over the rocky, unstable ground, as well as the items that had fallen from her supply bags as the horse had run. It was a long, endless tunnel of darkness. She could see a spot of light that looked different to that emitted by the glow-worms. It seemed like a white dot at first. Sia knew it was surely coming from the sun.

Sia sprinted toward the beaming light. She could see more white light breaking through the end of the cave. *This is the way out!* Sia pressed forward, despite the noise of the hag closing in on her, just inches behind. The old hag spread her mouth open wider than before, tearing her own face further open from ear to ear. She was prepared to devour Sia whole.

Sia swung the ivory bow over her shoulder to her chest, and pulled out two arrows from the case behind her. She drew the bowstrings back, turned, and released the silver arrows into the old hag's terrifying mouth. The silver-tipped arrows sizzled inside the old hag's mouth, and she choked, but it didn't slow her down. Sia looked extremely disturbed, and she hurried toward the light.

A horse's neigh came from just outside the cave, giving Sia the courage to keep going. She knew the sound of her own horse, Dawb. White mist curled out of Sia's mouth. The cold air was thick enough that she could see her own breath now. She was near the end. She stumbled out into the light.

Dawb charged at Sia and hiked up his front legs into the air. Sia leaped out of the way. With a mighty push, Dawb launched the old hag back into the darkness. The hag's screams vibrated through the cave.

The old hag stood up slowly. Her eyes burned with hatred for Sia. The horrid hag stepped forward, but stopped just short of the sunlight. She seemed to be afraid of the sun. She stayed in the shadows and gave Sia an evil grin. Blood still gushed from her torn cheeks and dripped from her severed hand. Defeated, the old hag slowly backed away into the darkness.

Sia shook off her fear. She turned to the horse, thankful for his help. Sia led the horse away from the cave and continued her journey.

CHAPTER 12
MAO-HLUB

The new world they had stumbled upon seemed like a peaceful one. Butterflies fluttered in the air. Fresh morning dew hung from the tips of flowers in the fields. Sia and Dawb came to the top of a hill after traveling a short distance. Sia gazed down on the peculiar land that lay below. A field of large brown and red mushrooms stood like small houses on a bed of vibrant moss.

"I've been to strange places. This is stranger." Sia wasn't sure where they were. Sia rode the horse through the giant mushroom field. She studied one of the red mushrooms as she approached it. Her eyes crinkled inward. The red mushroom had two slits in the middle of the cap. "Strange," said Sia.

Suddenly the slits on the mushroom cap opened. A pair of eyes stared back at her. Sia gasped. Alarmed, the horse reared up, nearly stomping at another mushroom. The mushroom blinked at him. The horse whinnied.

Sia steered the horse to the side before he almost smashed into the next living mushroom. She patted the horse on the side.

"Shh. Don't be afraid." She took a red sash from her waist and tied it around the horse's eyes, "Be brave. It's just for a little while." Sia continued riding.

All the mushrooms were watching her now.

"I pray they do not have mouths," Sia said, gathering her courage. The strange land seemed to stretch for miles ahead. The sunset painted the sky a gold and pink color. She proceeded with caution as she navigated through the mammoth, maze-like fungi.

When the night arrived, the sky and land were pitch-black. Sia and her horse rode into a wall. Sia felt the surface with her hand. It was soft like a blanket. It was the wall of a mushroom cap. She steered the horse in a different direction, and it was not long before they hit another mushroom. "It's just the mushrooms. We keep walking into them," said Sia.

Then, like magic, beams of light began to radiate around them. The light came from the mushrooms they had bumped into. It quickly became a full domino effect, scattered and random, a lovely light show. The mushroom caps glowed in the dark underneath the moonlight, as though they were communicating with one another in patterns. They lit up the field and showed the cleared paths for Sia and the horse to take. She steered Dawb while she looked around in complete awe and amazement. Fireflies rose from the ground, drawn to the fungal lighthouses.

Finally, the field of mushrooms was behind them. "Another forest," Sia sighed. She reached for the red sash around the horse's eyes, but paused. The night sky had lightened up to shades of blue.

Sia looked behind them and her eyes caught something moving in the air above the mushrooms.

Antlers. Deer-like. More antlers were scattered throughout the mushroom field. It puzzled Sia; she hadn't seen them on their way through. The antlers rose above the tip of the mushroom caps, holding Sia's full attention. "The heads of deer?" Sia thought out loud. "No, they're larger. Elks. That's normal. Elks are normal animals."

The heads of the elks grew higher. Sia pulled her hand back from the sash; she wouldn't allow the horse to be frightened again. Instead, she reached for the arrows behind her and positioned the ivory bow.

The mysterious creatures stepped out from behind the large mushrooms. They had thin fur coats and stood on long hooves. Elks with the body of men. Outlandish mythical beings. They stood together as a tribe and watched Sia, wondering if she was a threat or not. Sia didn't see them as a threat. She lowered the bow and arrow, turned her gaze away, and gently urged the horse to go a little faster into the next foreign forest.

After they had ventured deeper into the forest, Sia removed the sash from the horse's sight. "I know, it's another forest," she said. The horse tried to turn back, whinnying. "No, not that way." Sia spoke softly, "We've come this far, don't be afraid."

She found four scratch marks on the side of the horse where the old reins would have lain. Dawb's beautiful white coat was torn and crusted with dried blood. It was a sore sight for Sia.

She felt responsible. She took a deep breath, uncertain of the danger they would face before she could reach the highest peak.

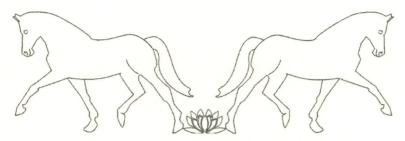

The sun was high in the sky, and it felt like the hour of noon to Sia. She and Dawb continued onward without a dirt path or trail to help navigate the way. No one had ever traveled this way, or at least none had in a long time. Sia and the horse were deep in the forest, and they were weary. They slowed down a little. Sia got down carefully from the horse, cracking the bones in her hands. "We'll stop here and rest till the sun is not so high or hot." Sia positioned the horse next to a tree.

The horse hesitated; he seemed fearful of the area.

"It's just a tree." Sia stroked the horse's side. "I'll be right here." She waited until the horse settled to the side of the tree. Sia leaned against the trunk and shut her eyes. It was quiet, no birds or crickets were nearby.

The forest floors shimmered. Rays of light shone upon the two of them, making Sia squint. She opened her eyes. It was hours past noon. The light fell at an angle through the cracks between the branches. The horse was awake too, standing tall, and he seemed to be in better shape than before. The blue tiger fur was still firmly tied to the small wooden wagon behind the horse. Sia was surprised to find a small woven sack among the blue fur. The sack was torn open, and there was clearly something left inside it.

Sia reached into the sack and pulled out an apple. She fed the apple to the horse. She reached inside the bag again and found that there was one more apple left. Sia bit into the side of the second apple, and then she gave the rest of it to the horse. He gobbled it up quickly. Sia brushed the horse's mane and told him, "That's all we have. Looks like we lost all our food in the cave. I must look for food."

Someone grabbed Sia's arm. Sia looked down and saw long, hairy fingers around her forearm squeezing so tightly that she felt her arm would soon break. She tried to break loose, but couldn't. The bushy creature tilted its head to the sky and let out a heavy peal of laughter through his big, wide mouth.

The horse was startled. Dawb kicked at the tall, hairy figure. The creature fell on its back, losing its grip on Sia's arm. It tried to snatch her again, but Sia ducked, and the hairy monster seized the ivory bow instead. Sia crawled away and left the bow with the monster. The bushy, brown creature struggled to roll over or get up from the forest floor. It wobbled and wobbled powerlessly.

Sia climbed onto the horse, and they rode off as fast as possible. She looked back at the gigantic half-ape and half-man-like creature. The hairy stranger was still teetering from side to side, helpless. Sia felt pity for the large ape-man, but she suddenly remembered: *they eat humans*. Then she suddenly realized that she had encountered a creature from the tall tales: the Mao-Hlub. "We met one." Sia laughed away her nerves. "I met a Mao-Hlub!"

What she saw next soon shut her up. Hidden behind a majestic grandmother tree was another Mao-Hlub. It made eye contact with Sia, staring at her awkwardly. Sia and the horse passed this creature quickly. She spotted another Mao-Hlub further down the path, also camouflaged behind a tree that looked similar to its shabby deep brown coat. Another pair of curious eyes stared at Sia. It had become clear to Sia that this place was their homeland, and she was the outsider passing through. She looked at her bruised arm and was relieved it was not broken.

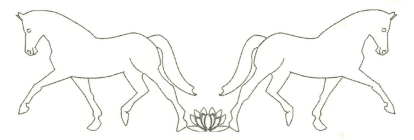

Sia and her horse arrived at a hill, overgrown like a jungle. They had traveled on for days, and it had affected their health and mood in the worst ways; both were weak and slowly losing their optimism. The horse moved slowly and was unable to lift his head. He was a perfect reflection of Sia. She soon fell off the horse, exhausted from starvation and dehydration.

A creature approached. It was a young deer, gracefully trotting past Sia and Dawb. Sia heard the splashing of water. There were more deer, and the sounds of small animals gathered around to drink nearby. She pushed herself off the ground and went after the sound of wildlife and water. Dawb followed behind her.

In just a short distance, beyond a bushy layer of tall grass and giant leaves, Sia discovered a small hidden paradise with a beautiful pond. She watched the harmonious interactions between the pond and peaceful animals. Flowers bloomed around the edges. The water sparkled on the surface. It was alluring.

Sia moved toward it, weak and trembling. The horse appeared to sense that something was wrong, and nudged Sia's shoulders. Then he neighed loudly at Sia, but she ignored him. Sia went straight to her knees at the edge of the pond. She began to fill a gourd with water and wet her hands. "It's warm," she said. The horse neighed at her again. The ground rumbled. The horse was frightened, and finally bit onto Sia's cloak, yanking her back forcefully. Startled, Sia shouted. She got up and almost lashed out at the white horse, but then *thump*. The young deer flopped to the ground, foaming at the mouth. The animals around the pond fell one by one. Birds scattered away and dropped dead in midair. The ground rattled and shook. Cracks formed in the earth.

Sia got on her horse and raced away as the ground beneath them split open. The tall green grass slid toward the water, and the pond folded inward like a large fly-trap, taking all the dead and dying animals inside it. The pond itself was a living creature, a carnivore. Black fungus and moss covered its rocky outer shell.

Glancing back, Sia couldn't believe her eyes. She tossed the gourd away and looked at her horse. Dawb had saved her life.

Later that day, they had traveled far beyond the dangerous living pond, and Sia was on her feet, trying to lead the worn-out horse. She was dirty, dried up like a raisin, and so was the horse. The forest was growing thin, allowing more light to come through the trees. They stumbled into a deep flourishing valley between the mountains.

Sia looked at the sparkles of light on the ground. It was a river, reflecting the light. Birds soared by and touched the surface of the gently flowing water. The birds flew off and lived. This water was safe. Sia pulled Dawb along to reach the water. They both drank from it, gulp after gulp without lifting their heads, until their bellies were filled, and they felt alive again. "Drink as much as you can," Sia told the horse. "We will rest here tonight."

That night, they rested by a tree near the river. Sia built a fire and fed sticks of wood into the crackling flames. Two medium-sized fish were skewered onto the silver tipped arrow and were cooked over the fire.

After the much-needed meal, Sia went to wash her hair and face in the river. The cool breeze brushed against her skin. She glazed into the night sky. Thousands of stars shone back at her, but none of them compared to the silver full moon that hung near the earth. *Beautiful.* She admired the grand design of the night sky and knew in her heart that there was something even greater than all of the beauty and mystery around her. She felt alone and small underneath the cosmic sky. Loneliness scared her more than anything she had encountered.

"Ancestors," Sia whispered. "Are you there?" The thought of her deceased brother saddened her. "Xiong, are you watching over me? Are you with father?"

She noticed the sound of water splashing lightly a short distance behind her. The horse stood on the shore and drank. Dawb looked well; his dirty coat was clean and white again.

A little later, Sia was drying herself by the fire. She looked at the horse, he was her only companion. "Who knew our earth is stranger than the tall tales," Sia said to him. "Is it strange that I am on this journey alone with a horse?"

The horse nudged her. "I know, I know," Sia said. "You're smart. Smarter than most men. Dawb, do you like your name? I named you after your white coat. You were the smallest horse on the farm. The horse breeder didn't think you were worth much, especially after your mother died. You weren't able to run like the rest of the horses. None of that mattered to me because when I saw you, I fell in love with you right away. I took you home and named you Dawb. White, beautiful, and strong, like your mother. She was from the wild. I never knew a horse could be so brave, and human."

She paused, then said, "I had a brother, Xiong, and he protected me like you do." She leaned her head on Dawb's side and rested her eyes. Soon, she was fast asleep.

CHAPTER 13
THE SOLDIER

Sia heard a deep masculine voice. "Young lady, wake up."
Sia opened her eyes. Dawb was missing.

"Where's my horse?" She was in the same place where she had fallen asleep, but she was disoriented.

The stranger in front of Sia wore black metal armor over dark leather. He bore seals and weapons that looked ancient. He was a soldier with a handsome face. Covered in dirt and scuffs, he appeared to have been in a long, rough battle.

"I must take you somewhere safe," said the soldier. He was out of breath, holding his helmet in one hand and a fierce iron sword in the other. His eyes were intense, yet genuine.

"Come with me," he said, and quickly put his sword in its sheath. Then he grasped her arm, ran, and pulled her into a magnificent willow tree. They were hidden underneath the crown in the shallow, hollow center of the grandmother tree. The blue-green leaves swayed on droopy branches like soft curtains. The great willow tree was a wise witch, weeping and sweeping her secrets with the breeze.

Sia couldn't take her eyes off this man as he looked at her. His build was taller and stronger than any man she had seen. "This is not happening," Sia said out loud to herself, trying to stop herself from panicking.

Suddenly, an arrow flew right by Sia, taking a strand of her hair. She lost her balance and fell forward. The soldier drew his sword and swung the blade just in time to counter the next arrow, splitting it down the middle. She fell onto his chest and saw the green sash around his waist. Without hesitation, he lifted her into his arms and ran straight past the willow tree, headed for a stone wall covered with thick green vines. All Sia could do was shut her eyes and hope she wasn't going to die.

The loud stampede of an army thundered across the land behind Sia and the mysterious, handsome soldier. The noise of men shouting and fighting surprised Sia.

Darkness. Sia scanned the stone walls. "What's happening?" asked Sia. Her eyes were adjusting. It was clear she was in a small cave.

"It's an ambush," the handsome soldier told her. "Stay here. I'll come back for you when it's safe." He ran forwards and pitched into battle.

The clashing of swords outside the cave filled Sia with terror. She felt like the rocky walls were caving in around her.

"Without my horse, how do I continue? Xai's skin is with my horse," Sia said out loud. It made little sense to her. "Dawb wouldn't just leave me. I must find them." She ran out of the cave, and went back into the willow tree, trying to stay hidden. She walked through the cluttered blue-green leaves, and pushed a section of vines to the side.

Sia found a battlefield. She came to a halt. Were her eyes deceiving her? Men lay dead on the ground by the hundreds, maybe thousands. Black armor and silver armor lay among the bloody mess. She scanned the piles of lifeless bodies. Tears swelled up in her eyes and fell. The image of humans dismembered and dead in the dirt shook her to her bones. She had only heard stories of war, but seeing it was a terror of its own.

Sia stepped out from the willow tree, cautiously. Her knees buckled. Fear overwhelmed the muscles in her legs, turning her calves into soft rice cakes.

Swords continued to strike and spark in the near distance. Sia turned to see five men fighting against one; five men in silver armor striking and launching swords at one black-armored man. She couldn't see their faces well. The fight lasted a minute more. They were no match for the man in the black armor. He swiftly cut them down to pieces. Sia watched the last head fall from a silver-armored soldier. The black-armored man had won.

The standing soldier turned to face her, and took a step toward her. Frightened, Sia bent down and picked up a random weapon; it was a spear. She had never used a spear before. Sia changed her mind, dropped the spear, and pulled the nearest sword from the ground. Sia noticed that the blade was smeared with blood.

Then, she saw the perfect weapon, it was a bow and a case of arrows between dead bodies. Sia switched weapons again, taking the bow from the cold hands of a dead soldier. She tightly gripped the bow and drew back an arrow. This felt natural for her. Sia walked backward, retreating into the old willow tree for her own safety.

The blade of a sword moved the long willow branches aside to make way for the black-armored man. The leaves swung shut behind him. The man was in Sia's view now. It was the soldier who had saved her earlier.

"You know how to use that?" There was a fresh cut over his brow.

"Yes," replied Sia confidently, the metal arrowhead aimed at his neck. His stern expression made her hands tremble. She had seen what he had done and could do, but she steadied her hands.

The soldier put his sword away. "I won't hurt you. I promise." Slowly, he reached for the bow. His face was splattered with blood. His armor had cuts in multiple places, and his side was bleeding out onto the green sash.

Sia felt sorry for him. Her gut told her to trust him. She lowered the bow and arrow. *What am I doing?* She clutched the weapon tightly.

The soldier took the bow and arrow from her, and set them down to the side. He held out his left hand to her, and it was bloody, and missing a finger, the pinky. "Come with me," he said urgently. "We must leave this place."

"I can't leave. Not without my horse," replied Sia.

"No one will come and help us. There's no food or medicine. I won't make it very far if we don't leave now."

"Go without me," said Sia. "I have to find my horse; it's important."

The handsome soldier liked her willful spirit. He reached for her hand, but she ignored him and stepped to the side.

Arrows entered the willow vines close to them and blazed through to the other side without harming them. They were being attacked again. The soldier embraced Sia to protect her. He thrust her against the bark of the willow tree and shielded her with his body. "What's more important than your life?" the soldier demanded. His eyes stayed on hers, even when she looked down to avoid him.

Sia's heart raced. "My husband's."

"Those words cut deeper than a sword." The soldier backed away from Sia to give her space. He was jealous, which made him more certain of his feelings. "If I live, I want to marry you."

Sia was baffled. "I, I'm…" She blushed.

"Married," he acknowledged, but it didn't change the way he felt about her. "You could run away with me."

"I can't, and I won't." Sia moved away from the tree, looking for an escape route.

"Why not?"

"I love him."

"Why do you love him?"

"I'd like to leave, now."

"Answer me first. Why do you love him?"

"We chose each other. I would choose him again," said Sia.
"I have…I followed my husband into the afterlife and brought him
back with me, body and soul. And now I will do everything I can
to keep him alive. So get out of my way, please."

"I've never been more envious," said the soldier. He
slammed the sword down behind Sia, and placed his arms around
her, close enough to hold her.

It was an intimate and awkward moment for Sia. She
should be angry, but she held back, because he was not quite
giving her a normal hug. Sia looked over her shoulder. He had tied
his green sash to the handle of his sword, and tied the other end
around her waist. Sia realized what had happened; she was tied to
the sword, bound by the soldier's green sash. "What are you
doing?" asked Sia.

The soldier made a second knot. "In another life I shall find
you first before any other man. Wait for me."

"You're mad."

"Enchanted." His voice was gentle, yet filled with so much
passion.

"Bewitched?" Sia wasn't convinced.

"I have defeated many witches, and none of them had the
power you do."

"Please stop talking like that."

The soldier chuckled. "As you wish."

"Don't smile like that either."

"I can't help it. You have cast that kind of…spell over me."

"Stop your flirting. We're in a battlefield, people are dead, and I have to—"

"Be careful. If you intend to keep going, then I must inform you that there's a warrior here who has slain dragons. She's more dangerous than the army she sent. Her name is Poj Rhawv Sab Ceeb (P-aw Ter Sha Cheng)."

"A woman warrior…" Sia asked, amazed. "You've seen her?"

"I fought her," confessed the soldier in a cold, serious tone. "This is the border just outside her land. No man has ever entered her kingdom and returned. Emperors and their armies have died here. You should not go any further."

"I can't stop here. Not now."

Those words made the soldier fall more deeply for her. He made a third knot around her waist. "I want you to live, but this is a place that none have ever survived to talk about."

"You can't keep me here. I can easily untie myself."

"It's not to keep your body here, it's to keep your soul here."

"What do you mean?"

"It's an old belief. You don't have to understand."

"I can't allow my soul to remain here."

"Just until I can be with you."

"You can be with any woman."

"I desire you, a woman who makes her own path."

"We've just met."

"Yet, it's like I've been waiting for you for a thousand years. I can wait one more lifetime. I would wage war for you. I would search the world and beyond for you. And I will never feel alive until I am with you." The soldier's voice echoed like a spell. "Wait for me."

The light wind circled them like whispers. He was invoking a powerful force. For a moment, Sia found herself mesmerized by the attractive soldier and his captivating words. Still, she rejected him. "I won't make promises to you."

The soldier simply smiled and wished her well, "Stay warm. It gets cold here. Stay safe. Death comes in strange ways."

Suddenly, a strong wind whirled around them both, brushing Sia's hair in front of her face and covering her eyes. An unseen force swept the soldier away beyond the blue-green leaves of the great, old willow tree.

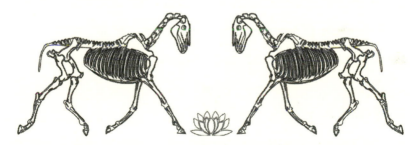

Sia jolted awake. It had been a dream. The fire in front of her had burnt out and turned to ashes. Dawb, her noble horse, was still there, wide awake, and waiting for Sia. She took a breath of relief.

It was just a dream. The soldier was a dream.

She rubbed her tired eyes and stood up, but something yanked her waist back. She looked down. There at her waist was the deep green sash, tied in three knots. She glanced behind her. There was an iron sword, the sword from the dream, planted in the dirt and bound to the green sash. It dawned on Sia that this was more than a dream. *The only thing missing is the willow tree.*

Sia remembered the soldier's voice. "It's keeping your soul here." Those words echoed in her head. She untied herself from the green sash and pulled the sword from the ground. She looked around, and saw the old willow tree in the near distance, standing in plain sight. *Why hadn't she noticed it before?*

Sia walked towards the willow tree. With each step she took, she recalled scenes from her dream. The soldier. His gaze. His hands. His smile. His energy lingered like a force surrounding her while she entered the space beneath the willow tree, almost seducing her. Everything was replaying in slow motion in her mind's eye. The sound of the vines swaying from side to side was hypnotic. It was all very alluring, and it reminded her of the short romance that had manifested in her dream.

Sia dug her nails into her own palm, drew blood, and snapped back to reality. *I'm not dreaming right now.*

Sia moved onward and arrived at the stone wall with leaves draped over it. She reached out and moved away the leaves. It was dark inside. She chopped at the leaves and branches to clear the path. Beams of light shone into the cave. Sia pressed forward, one step at a time. Something caught her eye. A body was hunched over by the wall. His skull leaned forward in the helmet. The skeleton was missing a finger bone.

Sia set the sword and green sash in front of the soldier's remains. She took a moment of silence. Then she spoke sincerely. "I don't know your name, but I am here to return your things. Please accept them back and do not follow me. I will not allow my soul to be tied down anywhere. Do not follow me." She stood up, but the sword snagged the end of her dress and shredded it. Sia realized she needed to do more. She crouched to face the skeleton and spoke to him again. "It must have been lonely to die here by yourself. You don't have to stay here in this place anymore. Death is not the end for you." She was speaking from experience.

The light wind breezed through the sweeping branches underneath the willow tree. It was now sunset hour. Dawb, stood underneath the willow tree with Sia. They both stared at a fresh mound on the ground, a grave. Sia plunged the sword down into the earth. The green sash was wrapped and tied over the handle of the old blade.

"Find peace. Find rest. Find reincarnation," said Sia to the buried soldier. Then Sia patted the neck of the white horse, "Come along, Dawb. I shall never speak of this to a living soul. No one would believe me." Sia led Dawb away from the gravesite of the fallen soldier.

CHAPTER 14
THE PAST

Sia and Dawb reached the foothills at the bottom of a range of mountains that seemed to stretch on endlessly. A rich jade bamboo forest covered the ground. Sia peered into the field of tall green stalks; they were feathery and flimsy, bending with the wind. This place reminded Sia of a time from her past.

Three years earlier...

The bamboo forest sprouted out of the ground like gigantic grass, a peaceful grove of trunks moving with the breeze under the cloudy sky. The sound of footsteps approaching from the distance startled Sia. Her eyes searched in the direction of the noise. She picked up a small knife from the pile of chopped bamboo trunks and hid it behind her back, inside the black cloak that covered her shirt and pants. She was dressed like a man. Though her hair was tied, it was still a mess.

The stranger came into view. It was Xai. He wore a small bag draped over his shoulder and pulled an empty wooden wagon. He was a traveling merchant. They looked at each other in silence, first with caution, then with curiosity. They both appeared to be around the same age. Sia's guarded expression softened, and she felt relieved. To her, he didn't look threatening, and to him, she looked like a young man with an innocent face. Besides, Xai was observant, and he noticed that the young stranger appeared to have been robbed of all their belongings.

Sia's exposed palms were blistered, most likely from being overworked. Xai was bothered by the young stranger's poor condition.

Perhaps this young man has had a difficult time surviving in the wilderness, he thought to himself.

Xai saw that the young stranger was barefoot and bleeding from the heels. He noticed a silver-plated clasp connected to a jade moth penned on black cloak over the clothes. The young man looked important.

Something was not right.

Xai slowed down, almost to a stop. "Are you lost?" he asked.

"No," said Sia, trying to seem tough.

"Do you need help?"

"I have no money to pay you."

"Where are you going?" The way he spoke matched his gentle appearance.

Sia let down her guard a little more and answered. "Home, with my brother."

"Where is your home?"

She hesitated, and he saw it on her face.

Xai kindly asked, "Is it far from here?"

"Ten days."

"Ten days." Xai glanced at her raw feet. "Can you make it without shoes?"

"Yes…"

Xai understood, nodded politely to her, and continued on his way.

"But my brother won't make it." There was a cry for help in her tone.

Xai stopped and asked, "Where is he?"

Sia paused. She wanted to trust him, but she regretted speaking to him at all. Xai recognized the doubt in her eyes. He assured her, "I only want to help. You don't have to worry about paying me. I sold every scroll and brush that I made this year. I'm content."

Sia had no choice. She had to trust him. No one else had come past her on the path, and it had been days. She led the way to a place nearby.

Bamboo branches covered a body, a pale young man. Xai quickly knew that this young man was already dead. The deceased

115

brother was laying on a poorly crafted raft that had to be dragged, and the raft itself was in need of repair. It was obvious now how Sia got the grazes on her palms.

"How long have you been traveling with him like this?"

"Three days," replied Sia.

Xai held back his tears before they could fall. "I have an empty wagon," he said. "Allow me to help get you both home."

It was a relief to receive his offer, but then Sia's vision became blurry. Her head felt heavy, and her eyes rolled back. Everything went black, and she fell to the ground with a loud thump. Xai rushed to her side. She was hot to the touch, and he felt her forehead.

He leaned over her. "You have a fever."

Sia didn't respond.

Xai asked, "Where is your home?"

Sia's eyes were closed, but she mumbled, "Moth... Mountain."

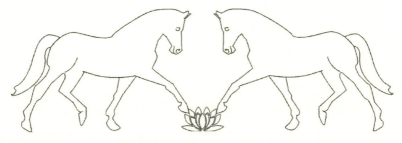

By the time Sia opened her eyes again, she was sitting up against a large bamboo trunk. Her hands were bandaged. The cloth matched the color of the red sash around the stranger's waist. She noticed that her shirt was loose. She remained calm as she attempted to figure out what had happened.

Xai took off the last remaining portion of the red sash from his waist and ripped the cloth in half. He was on his knees as he tended to the wounds on her feet. Sia felt uncomfortable with a man that close to her, but the shooting pain from the soles of her feet outweighed her conservative nature.

Xai lifted his head to see Sia looking back at him. "You're awake."

Sia looked away from him. She felt embarrassed. "Was I asleep for long?"

"Not long. You fainted. You're exhausted, and you have a fever."

She pushed herself up, but fell back down. Xai caught her arm, but she pushed him away firmly, telling him, "I'm fine now."

"I know you're a woman." Xai wanted to address the obvious.

"If you tell anyone—"

"I won't tell. I promise."

He gave her some space. Sia fixed her shirt and put her clothes back in order.

"Forgive me for…" Xai glanced at her loose shirt. "I didn't see much. And I stopped right away, as soon as I saw," he stopped himself. "Nothing. I saw nothing."

"Please do not tell anyone."

"Trust me. I won't tell anyone if you don't want me to."

Sia grew quiet.

"You're from Moth Mountain," Xai told her. "The hidden kingdom." He tried to hide his excitement. "Outsiders can never find it."

Sia's expression changed. She didn't like it that he knew so much about her. *Does he want to find Moth Mountain?* She warned him, "There'll be arrows in you before you can even get close to it."

"I see," said Xai. "Does Moth Mountain still have a royal family?"

"Why do you ask?"

"Well, everything about Moth Mountain is a secret. And there are only a few Hmong kingdoms left. Our people have been at war with other nations for centuries. People have a better chance of survival living near a haunted forest than in a city or a kingdom."

"Haunted forests are just stories to scare people; otherwise, you wouldn't be traveling alone. Would you? If the forests are haunted?" asked Sia.

He stayed quiet, unsure of how to answer. He liked the way she talked.

Sia continued, "War is real, and Moth Mountain is a place of peace. We are a free people, and we want to remain that way. Not all outsiders will understand."

"Even with all the mystery, when people from my village hear about Moth Mountain, we see it as a perfect place. Your people are held in the highest regard. Everyone is rich, educated, talented," said Xai. He looked at her and added, "And beautiful. I hope Moth Mountain can stay hidden for a few more centuries, with or without a royal family."

His words surprised her. "Yes," said Sia. "Moth Mountain has a royal family."

"So, shall we get you somewhere close enough to be seen and avoid being killed?"

"I know a path. You won't be able to go the entire way."

"I understand. As long as we both live, we can both make it home."

Sia felt relieved, like a heavy boulder had been lifted off her shoulders. "Will you help carry my brother onto the wagon?"

"Yes. Of course."

The first two days passed smoothly as they walked side by side through the valley. Her pace was slow, but he was patient. They filled most of the daytime hours with awkward silence, avoiding eye contact. Sia liked the quiet company, and so did Xai. He caught her looking back at him now and then, and it made him forget the heavy wagon behind him.

I KNOW A PATH

They stopped to rest often, and one time, when Sia dozed off, he painted on the back of her right hand with a small brush and black ink. Just as he finished the artwork, she woke up to the sight of his face. Sia backhanded his forehead, it was a natural response. He shouted, rocked backwards, and fell on his butt. She drew a fist at him, but then Xai held up the ink and brush. "I didn't mean to scare you," said Xai.

The seriousness on Sia's face changed the moment she saw the black ink on his forehead. She looked down to her hand and then back to his forehead, and chuckled. "It's on your head."

He touched his forehead and felt the ink. He laughed.

"Why did you paint on my hand?" asked Sia.

"I apologize."

Sia looked at the symbol. "Why did you choose a house?"

Xai was embarrassed. "It's what I have been working and saving for."

"You want to buy a house?"

"I want to build a home." He cleared his throat and turned away to wipe his forehead. "Shall we leave now?"

"Yes," Sia looked at the symbol on her hand once more.

Later that night, the large silver moon was nearly full and appeared close to the earth. They had entered another bamboo forest. The two sat beside a warm fire. There were bamboo shoots stuffed inside short bamboo trunks, cooking over the fire.

Sia was wrapped in a cotton blanket. "Are you sure you won't be cold?" she asked.

"The fire will keep me warm enough," replied Xai. "Are you sure you don't want to wear my shoes?"

"It's kind of you, but if you become injured, we won't get very far. I'm already in your debt." She tilted her head to the night sky.

Xai's eyes followed her gaze. They admired the thousands of silver stars. A star shot across the sky. Another falling star followed. Then another, and another. It was a meteor shower, blazing through the night sky with thousands of light-trails. *Breathtaking.* They watched in silence and marveled at the unexplained phenomenon. Xai stole looks at Sia now and then. She met his gaze, and they both smiled at one another. They both felt the attraction, and it also made them shy.

"How much further do we travel now?" asked Xai.

"Two more days north," replied Sia. "Remember, once we've climbed to the top of the red mountain, you can't go any further."

"I'll remember." He tried to find something else to say. "The sky always makes me feel small."

Sia remained silent.

"When I was younger, my grandfather would tell me stories as old as the stars," Xai said. "I asked a lot of questions as a child. Who put all the stars in the sky? And why do they only come out a night? My grandfather would say, *'We are not meant to know everything, but if we truly seek an answer, we may find more than we can comprehend.'* He was a wise man, and superstitious."

She liked that story, and her smile encouraged him to keep talking about his grandfather.

"He and I were traveling back home from the trade city, and he suddenly fell ill. As he was dying, he called to his father to bring him home."

Sia looked curious.

Xai explained, "You see, he believed that if he were to die far from home, then his soul might remain lost, and wander the land, so he called on his late father to guide his spirit home."

Sia wanted to compliment his story, but she didn't know what to say.

"You're often quiet," teased Xai.

"I hear it's a good trait, for a girl," replied Sia.

"Not always. If you hadn't spoken up, I wouldn't have been able to help you." Xai grew curious and asked, "What happened to your brother?"

"We are messengers for the Emperor of Moth Mountain. Our kingdom does not want war. Apparently, the other side does."

"You're a royal messenger? Every position in the royal court is for men. You're a—"

"A woman. Yet, at first sight, you did not know. And you treated me as your equal."

"Why would you pretend to be a man?"

"I've been pretending to be a boy most of my life, so that my parents didn't have to trade me to survive. I came from a small village, and only boys can work for silver. A girl can be sold, but not paid. I will not be bought as a slave or a wife. How can anyone measure the worth of their daughter by silver or cattle?" She sighed. "I apologize. I don't mean to sound bitter. My mother loves me and my father was good to us. I understand and respect the tradition, but as a girl, putting a price or value on my life does not make me feel important...or human."

"I must admit, that is a strange tradition that I'm nervous about. My parents often pressure me to find a wife, and so I've been on journeys of trade year in and year out to prepare for land and marriage," confessed Xai. "I understand how you feel. It's tradition and respect between families. It is something older than us. We cannot define or defy it. Most of us honor it." He quickly felt embarrassed, and changed the subject back to her. "So, you weren't born on Moth Mountain."

"We moved to Moth Mountain after my father died. My mother has royal blood, so she could always go home. Working for the kingdom pays well, and it turns out I am just as fast as my brother at riding horses. Messengers always go out in pairs, and we work well together. Moth Mountain is not my birthplace, but after twelve years, it's become home."

Xai listened with the greatest interest, but he had to ask, "How did you survive, while your brother didn't?"

"Our orders were to deliver a message to another Hmong kingdom. When we arrived, it had already been destroyed. We rode into a trap, enemy soldiers surrounded us, and they forced us to make a choice. Only one messenger could return with their reply to the Emperor, but it was immediate death for the other messenger. My brother volunteered to die so that I could deliver the message… and live."

Xai felt bad. "Forgive me. I shouldn't ask any more questions."

"You were just curious, and you've been kind."

"I *am* curious," Xai continued. "What happened to your horse?"

Sia paused for a moment to hold back her emotions. Then she answered, "I traded the horse for my brother's body. At first, they laughed at me. Then I offered the silver I wore, the silver bow and arrows, and the sword with a silver case. I told them all I wanted was to bring his body back for burial. I thought they were going to punish me or kill me, but the general accepted the trade. He stripped everything valuable from my brother as well, and then told me that if I could carry his dead body, then I could have him. I left with my brother on my back, and their laughter slowly faded away. The men just watched in silence. They killed my brother, and then took pity on me."

"I'm sorry that happened to you. I'm sorry about your brother," said Xai with deep sadness in his tone.

"His name was Xiong."

"That's my grandfather's name." He looked down at her wrapped feet. "They took your shoes as well?"

"The general took them for himself."

"He must have small feet," added Xai. He immediately regretted saying such a flippant thing. He quickly spoke, "Forgive me. That was insensitive. I meant no offense."

Sia smiled, "I'm not offended."

Xai stated earnestly, "You don't ever have to wonder about your worth in silver or cattle. Your brother traded his life for you. That's how valuable you are."

Those words were bittersweet, good to hear, and hard to stomach. "I don't know how to tell my mother that her one and only son is dead," said Sia.

"Your mother will be proud of you both. Her son died for his sister, and her daughter is carrying him home for a proper funeral and burial. His soul can be put to rest, find the afterlife, or be reincarnated."

It grew still between them. The bamboo shoots had boiled over into the fire. Xai plucked them one by one from the fire and announced, "The bamboo shoots are safe to eat now." He handed her one, bouncing it from hand to hand.

"Why are you helping me?" asked Sia.

"It's human nature to help each other."

"You are more kind than most. Normally strangers wouldn't place so much trust in each other."

"I like you." It was more honest than the first answer.

Sia was speechless. It took her a second to ask him, "When did you start liking me?"

"The moment I knew you were a woman," confessed Xai. He held two bamboo trunks out to her, avoiding eye contact.

Sia reached for the bamboo trunks. "Thank you."

Their fingers touched for the first time. Neither one pulled back. Xai was fond of Sia, and he wasn't afraid to show it. She took the warm bamboo trunk from him and settled back down. Her cheeks were warmer than before, and she went back to avoiding eye contact. Now it was more awkward.

Xai ate slowly. He didn't feel hungry anymore, just nervous. It was not normal for him to admire someone so much that he felt like he was going to catch on fire. He met her eyes, and his chest felt like it would explode on the inside. He had to declare his feelings, "Sia—"

Sia suddenly collapsed and landed on her side. Her eyes were heavy.

Xai rushed over and grabbed her shoulders, shouting, "Sia!" Sweat covered her skin, and her lips were as pale as her face. He touched her forehead; she had a fever. The sound of his voice faded away as Sia closed her eyes.

The next morning, the warm sun danced on Sia's face. She opened her eyes to see her brother's face, but remembered he was dead. It crushed her inside, and she wanted to cry but stayed strong. Sia turned her face upwards and lifted her eyes to see the back of a man towering over her. She was on the wooden wagon, and Xai was pulling them up the foothills of what appeared to be a high mountain, filled with red flowers blooming on every inch of the ground.

Xai looked over his shoulder to see her looking up at him. "Just one more day. The kingdom is near." He smiled at her, sweat beading off his brows and down the side of his neck.

Sia didn't feel worthy of his kindness, but she was too weak to move. She closed her eyes

The next day, Sia lifted herself from the ground. Her elbows bent back and forth trying to support her upper body, and her arms felt like brittle sticks. She was lying on a thin layer of fabric. She sat up properly, still weak. She saw Xai's back. He was near, looking at the view behind a large tree, and he was without his long coat. She realized that she was lying on his coat right now.

The small wooden wagon was parked at the side, leaning by a tree. Sia's brother's body was carefully wrapped in the cotton blanket that she had been using the previous night.

Xai glanced over to discover Sia was awake. He was relieved, and it was obvious that he had kept a close watch on her.

"We're here," said Sia, amazed that they made it.

"Yes," replied Xai. "Now what happens?"

"I must go on my own now. If only I had a bow and arrow, I could send a message."

Xai went to his sack and pulled out a small bow and two arrows.

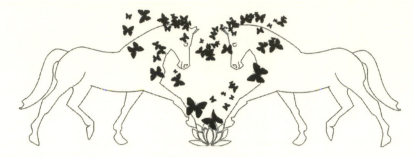

Moments later, Xai propped Sia up against a tree. They both stared at the sea of rich, blue-green mountains before them.

"How far do you think it will go?" Xai was intrigued.

"We shall see," said Sia. She poked the tip of the metal arrow into her pinky finger. Her finger bled onto the metal arrowhead, and she painted the blood in a straight line all the way down the arrow.

Xai watched in silence, astonished at the unusual message she was sending.

Sia drew the arrow back, pinpointed a location with her sharp eyes, and loosed the bowstring. The arrow went flying, soaring into the air and disappearing somewhere into the sea of mountains.

"Are all royal messengers this highly skilled?" asked Xai.

Sia was flattered, but said sadly, "They're all dead. My brother and I were the last ones, the youngest and lowest-ranked. One year of training, one year sending messages."

"I see," Xai felt slightly stupid. "What will happen next?"

"They'll come for me," Sia informed him.

"How do you know?"

"I know."

This felt like goodbye. Xai opened his mouth, but nothing came out. He was lost for words.

"Thank you, for all you've done for me," Sia thanked him.

Xai nodded. "I'm happy we met."

There was a brief moment of silence. Xai didn't want to part ways, and Sia felt the same. They stared at each other, waiting for the other to say something. The fleeting moment was ripping Xai's heart out, and he opened his mouth, but Sia spoke first.

"Let us meet again." Sia was saying goodbye.

"Let us meet again." There was sadness in his voice.

Xai turned away and saw the full moon. He paused, and turned to face Sia again. "I will come here, thirty days from now, on a full moon. And I will be here waiting, for as long as the moon is full...to meet you again."

"Why?"

"Because I'm convinced that you're the one for me. There's no one else for me."

"I…" Sia was lost for words. She had never experienced love like this. "I ride horses, which is forbidden for women. They say women cannot bear children if they ride horses. Doesn't that worry you?"

"No. I am more than content with you."

"I make weapons. I've never worked in the rice fields or grown anything in my entire life. I will not be a wife like others might. And more importantly, I value my freedom."

"You will always be free to live as you wish, with or without me. As for me, my wish is to build a home with you."

Sia wanted to reply, but for the first time in her life, she didn't know how. She couldn't encourage him, but she also had feelings for him. Her lips parted with nothing to say.

Xai understood her silence and said, "Let us meet again." He took another good look at her face before turning away. Those words lingered with Sia as she stopped herself from chasing after him.

CHAPTER 15
THE HIGHEST PEAK

*B*ack in the present…Sia and the white horse were at the foothills of some mountains. A bamboo forest covered the area. This time, her companion was a horse. "Just a few more days," Sia said out loud. She had gotten used to talking to herself, and the horse. She took a deep breath and kept moving forward.

They entered the forest of tall green giants. Dawb weaved through the bamboo trunks with Sia on his back. They were both hungry. Sia got off the horse and scanned the area. She spotted a small field of bamboo shoots.

In the evening, the two of them rested by a small fire. The warm, burning logs sparkled and popped, sending out a golden light into the cold night. Sia had dug a hole in the ground, deep enough to draw water up from the earth. She chopped down one bamboo trunk and sliced it up into shorter pieces. The small knife was getting dull. She peeled away the exteriors of bamboo shoots, split the soft core into small pieces, and stuffed them into the hollow ends of the short bamboo trunks. The soft bamboo shoots boiled over the fire.

The horse neighed at her. Dawb was starving and impatient. Sia glanced at him. "I know you're hungry, but the bamboo shoots need to boil longer. Otherwise, they could be poisonous."

Sia's eyes followed the bamboo trunks up to the sky. The stars were coming out. It was a rare sight to see. She felt small at the bottom of the soft, swaying trunks. There had been a moment like this for her years ago. It was with Xai, when they first met. The memory of the two of them flashed in her mind, both shy and happy to have each other for company.

It was daylight. Flakes of cotton-like snow fell over Sia and her noble snow-white horse. They were already on high ground. The horse was knee-deep in a blanket of snow. The two stared at the highest peak, at the mountains upon mountains. They were beyond the point of exhaustion.

Astonished, Sia softly said, "This is the highest place on earth." She stroked the side of Dawb's neck in a loving gesture, appreciating him. Sia saw that the skin on the back of her hand was dried and crackling. It was cold, and they were still only at the bottom of the mountain. She sighed. "If only you had wings, we could fly there and finish this journey sooner."

The horse nodded and carried along the route. The further they went, the more heavily the snow fell. There was no sun above them, just thick white clouds that stretched as far as the eye could see. The snow on the ground was waist-high on the horse, and he almost blended in with the white. Sia lost sight of the path in front of them. They had traveled into a dangerous storm. The blizzard escalated.

Sia jumped off the horse, trying to turn him around. She shouted, "Go back, Dawb!" She tried to release the wagon with the blue fur skin from the back of the horse, but he refused and cried loudly in response. The midnight-blue fur skin looked almost black now.

"Go back!" Sia tried a second time to untie the fur skin. She looked at her red hands, which were swollen and frozen. She could barely use her fingers. She got the ropes loose and tied the fur skin around her waist. Sia pushed the horse away, "Go!"

The horse neighed at Sia, refusing to leave her.

"You can't die here with me." Sia pushed him back the opposite way.

The horse neighed again and whinnied. Sia pushed him back, but the horse wouldn't budge.

The ground rumbled. Sia turned her head. Her eyes doubled in size. It was an avalanche; a mighty force of nature charging at

them, larger than any beast she had ever seen. She looked back to
the horse, and her eyes wept in fear. Sia wrapped her arms around
Dawb's neck and held him.

POOF. They both disappeared completely. The side of the
mountain was a smooth, pure white. Everything was quiet.

Suddenly, Dawb's nose emerged from the snow.
Something was pulling him out of the deep snow. There was heavy
breathing from above the snow. It was two husky horses, Yakuts.
They were furry, and the same breed as Dawb. The Yakut horses
pulled Dawb onto higher ground, and Sia's head broke the surface.

Sia gasped for air. They were alive.

Sia opened her eyes. The sunlight blinded her. Heavenly
light sparked between the two Yakut horses. Their silver-white
coats were longer than those of normal horses, with shaggy hair on
all four legs leading down to gray hooves. Sia looked at the
gorgeous creatures in awe. She cautiously reached for one of the
wild horses. Her fingertips touched the nose of the closest one.

She softly laughed and said, "Thank you."

She glanced at Dawb, who was bonding with the other
horse, meeting their wet noses together. Dawb turned back to Sia,
and somehow without a word, they both knew in their hearts that
the horse belonged with his own kind.

Sia took the small knife and cut the ropes from Dawb's
body. The horse was bare. Then, she pressed her forehead against
his and said, "I love you." A hint of sorrow vibrated from her
voice. She stepped aside and gently nudged him forward with her

hands. Sia watched as her loyal white horse took careful steps toward the wild Yakut horses. Dawb looked back at Sia, but she just smiled at him, willing him to keep going.

More wild horses appeared on the horizon: a herd of silver, gray, and white animals. The herd welcomed Dawb as he joined them. Sia watched in amazement as her truest friend pranced off with his tribe in perfect unison. Warm tears painted streaks on Sia's numb cheeks. She was happy for him.

The lovely moment passed. Sia was alone now. It was time for her to face the mountain on her own. She wrapped the ropes around her arms and hands and dragged the fur skin behind her. The snow was shoulder-deep, but she forced herself forward.

More snow fell. Sprinkles of snow floated around aimlessly. It didn't matter at this point. Sia braved the steady snowfall on the way to the top of the highest mountain. She pulled the deep-blue fur skin forward, pushed it with her back, and even rolled the ugly thing up the steep mountain. Then she dragged it behind her again. At one point, she tied the fur skin to her waist and shoulders. She took one heavy step after another.

The memory of those days when she first met Xai came to mind. She recalled the way the sweat had rolled down the back of his neck as he forced every ounce of his muscles to keep climbing uphill with her on the wagon. The reminder of his courage gave her the power to take the next step. The old image of the way Xai turned to look at her and smiled through the heavy burden pushed her to keep going. She thought of his earnest heart when Xai glanced over his shoulder to see her looking up at him.

The memory blurred into Sia's reality. It was as though he was there with her in the present, standing in the snow. Xai spoke. "Just one more day. The kingdom—"

"—is near," recited Sia, freezing, with her teeth chattering in the cold. She launched her legs into the snow and took another step, followed by another. The image of her husband suddenly vanished. She was alone. He was never really there with her on the snowy mountain.

Sia plopped down into the deep trail of snow, struggling to catch her breath. She lay on her back, leaning on the deep-blue fur skin. Snowflakes landed on her pale, frostbitten skin. She struggled to her feet and instantly fell back down again over the rolled-up fur skin.

Hundreds of tiny footprints marked the trail behind her. From a far distance, she must have seemed a blue and black speck on the wall of the great peak. Up close, Sia clawed her red fingers into the snow to stop herself from sliding down. The pain caused her to grunt. Her lips cracked, and warm blood washed her bottom lip a scarlet red color.

Sia gritted her teeth to keep them from chattering. The taste of iron felt hot on her tongue and then quickly grew cold. She got back on her feet and climbed further up the slope of the snowy mountain. Her legs were stiff and aching, and she rubbed them to help with the blood flow, but it was difficult to bend her elbows.

Sia lifted her head, and her eyes could see the horizon. She pulled herself up, dragging the fur behind her. Finally, out of strength and out of her mind, she reached the ground of the highest peak. She was standing in the clouds.

Sia cut the rope that bound her waist to the deep blue-fur skin, now covered in frost. She looked back at the way she had come. The falling snow had covered her tracks, filling in her recent footprints, and would eventually erase all evidence of her being there. Sia turned to look ahead. She stood tall at the highest place on earth, staring in wonder. The cold breath from her mouth didn't concern her anymore.

"The end of the world," said Sia. Never had she imagined that she would come to such a place as this. She watched her breath escape into the freezing air like soft smoke, and she shut her eyes to take in the moment. It was quiet. No wind. Not a sound.

The time had come. Sia rolled the fur skin to the other edge of the cliff. The scene that lay beyond the cliff was a deep pit of pure white landscapes that went on forever. It was another world entirely, a place of only ice and snow.

She inhaled, exhaled, and remembered the right words to speak. "If you all want your old possessions, come and claim them!"

Sia shoved the fur skin with all her might, pushing with her frostbitten hands. As soon as she saw it fall over the cliff, she scurried away. But Sia was a curious creature by nature. Soon, she slowed down, and her feet stopped moving. She was tempted to see what was happening to the fur skin. She paused, slowly turned her head, and looked over her shoulder.

A pair of pearl-white claws launched at her.

Sia instantly regretted what she had done, but it was too late. Two curved claws scratched her arms, peeling layers from her flesh, and stuck in the back of her left forearm. The claws were massive, the length of her hands. They were just claws, with no creature attached. Sia ran as fast as her short legs would take her. Her heart raced with adrenaline pumping through her veins and bleeding out her wounds. She didn't think she had any more strength left in her, but she needed to outrun whatever attacked her. She sprinted down the mountain, falling and tumbling, but she kept going until she reached the bottom of the mountain. She fell to her knees. Her arm had stopped bleeding, and the wounds had clogged up, but the claws were still firmly in place.

Her shoes were worn down and torn in places, and her toes peeked out, burned by the snow. She continued walking like this for miles. The sun was going down, and so was the last of Sia's strength. Her body was moving slower than her breath could escape her lips. She shivered and hugged herself to keep warm. She hadn't expected the journey back to be a potential death sentence.

Darkness fell. Sia tried to keep going. She crawled on all fours, pulling her own body along. Sia turned onto her back. She opened her dried, bleeding lips to catch the cotton-like snow. It melted on her tongue. The small, cold snowflakes could not quench her thirst. She felt as though she was dying.

Then a star shot across the sky, followed by another. More and more burning rocks burst through the purple and black night like they were all racing to a destination far away. It was a meteor shower. The incredible moment brought tears to Sia's eyes, streaking down from the corners and running over her temples. The image that crossed her mind was Xai; his face when they had last bid farewell. *Is this the end for me? I don't want to be a lost, wandering soul if I die here.* Her chapped lips opened, and she said, "Father...I'm ready to come home." The look in her eyes showed defeat.

The heavy clouds above Sia parted. Warm light shone over her. An image appeared in front of her. It was the face of a man. He had kind eyes. When he smiled, it made Sia feel like she was home. She knew him. The faintest whisper slipped from her lips, "Father."

"Don't sleep here, daughter," the man said.

"Father...take me home," pleaded Sia.

"I can help you only this once. Choose your words wisely."

This confused Sia at first. Then she thought of her husband and said, "I want to be with my husband, Xai."

The man in front of her melted into the cosmic light. It glowed brighter. Sia shut her eyes, blinded by the brightness and the power.

Blurred images flashed in front of her as she fell in and out of consciousness. Sia was in the clouds. The earth below was made up of miniature portions of forests, bamboo fields, lush valleys, sparkling rivers, and mountains spiking up like little furry pebbles.

Sia's face was pressed against something soft and white. The fine, white hair of the creature brushed her cheeks. Sia lifted her eyes to see the figure of a pearl-white head, a horse's head. Her voice was weak and low, "A flying horse…I'm dreaming."

"You are not dreaming. I am flying, and I am a horse." replied the flying horse. Her voice was strong and soothing.

"A talking horse," said Sia. She was shocked, but then again she was still only partly conscious.

"I prefer flying horse," corrected the horse. "I prefer you don't recall this event later. Hopefully your fever will help take this memory away."

"Why? Don't you want people to know you exist?" Sia stroked the mane of the flying horse. It was comforting to her while her sight was foggy, and many uncertain thoughts were coming up, and disappearing just as quickly.

"When the time is right."

"When will the time be right?"

"After I meet a prince. He's a little late, but when he arrives in this land, I will help him take the kingdom."

"Why?"

"It's my destiny," said the flying horse proudly.

"Why?"

"Because the prince, *that prince*, is favored by the fertility god." The flying horse sounded a little annoyed by Sia's questions. "I was created to help him."

"A fertility god." Sia was pleasantly surprised to discover that such a god existed. "I had a beautiful horse, like you. His name was Dawb. Can all horses talk?"

"I don't have all the answers," replied the flying horse. "I thought you would be asleep through the whole journey back home," the flying horse told her. "In fact, you are dreaming right now. So, you may shut your eyes in order to wake up because this is a dream."

Sia didn't question the flying horse. She softly responded, "I see." She wrapped her arms around the flying horse's neck, rubbed her head in its mane, and closed her eyes. "I thought you were my father, but you are a horse with a woman's voice." She mumbled, "Nothing makes any sense."

Then, as Sia was falling asleep, the tip of her toes skimmed the cold surface of some water below, where a huge scaly river dragon moved underneath the surface. She jolted awake.

The scaly river dragon came to the surface in a graceful manner. Its orange-gold scales shimmered in the moonlight like flakes of pure gold. The golden dragon and Sia saw each other as the horse flew by.

"What is that?" asked Sia, keeping her eyes on the large scaly creature in the river.

"You weren't supposed to see her," said the flying horse.

"Her?"

"A dragon princess."

"A dragon princess?" Sia rubbed her eyes, and looked again.

The golden dragon was still there, staring back at Sia.

"Yes, poor creature. Her father wants her to marry an orphan boy, a human."

"How is that possible?"

"Please fall asleep," said the flying horse. "Sleep."

Sia's eyes were heavy, and she couldn't keep them open. "Sleep."

The flying horse was casting a spell on Sia. She lay her head on the back of the horse.

"Sleep."

Sia's voice became a whisper, "Who sent you to help me?"

"Your ancestors and the gods," answered the flying horse. She went back to chanting, "Sleep. Sleep. Sleep."

Sia whispered, "Thank you, flying horse. I hope you meet your prince."

Her last words touched the flying horse in its core, but Sia wouldn't know it, for she was deep in slumber.

Back at the river, the golden dragon watched them soar far away, over the land. A curious creature, the golden dragon transformed into a human girl with long golden hair. She looked at her fingers, which were delicate and perfect. She peered into the reflection of the water to see a face staring back at her, identical to Sia's face. She smiled, content with her human face.

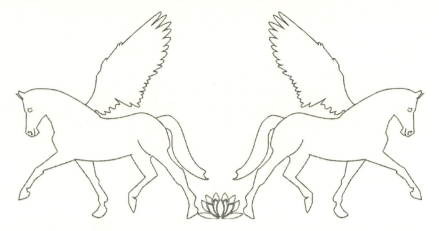

Some time later, Sia opened her eyes. Ruby apples hung over her. The smell of sweet apples came from above her and fresh blades of grass surrounded her cheeks. It was warm in this place. There was shade. She saw the black bird perched in the tree, staring back at her. "The black bird. Can you speak?" she asked and gave the bird a moment to reply. The black bird chirped, which told Sia that she was back in her world. She let out a soft sigh of relief. She looked at her shoes, and saw snow and dust on them. It was not a dream.

The sound of chickens clucking and pigs snorting came from nearby. Sia sat up and propped herself up on the tree trunk. Her knees buckled. She lost her balance and fell right into someone's arms. She looked to the side and met a pair of brown eyes. They belonged to her husband, Xai. She was home.

CHAPTER 16
HOME AGAIN

The sudden reminder of her injured arm made her jump up. Sia quickly hid her arm behind her back, afraid of what Xai would say after he had warned her not to look back. Everything she had endured remained on her physical body, including the wounds on her hands and the scabs on her bottom lip.

It was hard for Xai to see that his lovely wife had sustained such harm. He embraced her and held her tightly. "You've come home." Xai breathed in the scent of her neck. "I've missed you, wife."

Those words made Sia smile. "I have missed you, too."

He felt blessed, full of joy. He was overwhelmed with emotions, the greatest one was shame for sending his wife to do something he knew he could not accomplish. He thought to himself; *even though I wanted to, it was impossible for me to save myself.* "If it had been me, I would have met the same fate as the fur skin. If no one had gone on my behalf—"

"That is behind us now," said Sia.

"Forgive me," said Xai. "You have risked your life for mine once more."

"I would do it again," Sia replied with a smile. "If you live, I live with you. If you die, I die with you. Wherever you go, I'll go, too."

"Don't repeat such words. We're together now, that's all that matters." He wrapped his arms around her shoulders and escorted her home.

As they approached the hut, Xai grew suspicious of Sia's hidden arm and asked, "What's wrong?" He tried to reach for the arm, but she pulled away.

"Let me see your arm," Xai demanded.

Sia was afraid to show him, but she revealed her arm. The two white claws were wedged through her coat and flesh. Her forearm was healing, but it was crippled. Xai knew the claws belonged to giant beasts not of this world. He grabbed her injured arm, but gently. Xai took her straight inside the hut, charging towards the fireplace. Without warning, Xai shoved her injured arm into the mound of gray and black ashes. The claws fell right through Sia's arm. She gasped with panic, fearful that she had also lost her arm.

Sia pulled out her perfect arm. No exit wounds or scars. Only the tears in her coat and dress remained. It was a miracle. "Where did you learn to do that?"

"The knowing is inside of me, remember?"

"Of course, I remember now."

It was later that evening. They sat facing one another in silence.

Xai had an unsettling thought. *Is Sia really here?* He was paranoid. She seemed like an imposter to him, but he didn't know why. It was hard for him to hide his emotions, and he had a request for Sia. "Take a chicken and cook a meal for me. If you don't burn the food, then you are my wife. If you burn the food, you are not my wife."

Sia responded with a quiet nod. Her husband instantly gathered his instruments immediately and exited through the doorway.

Sia set the pot of water over the crackling fireplace. She took a basket of herbs and prepared the meal. Music came from the front yard, reaching her ears.

Sia turned to the open window, which framed her husband perfectly. Outside in the yard, Xai was playing the *qeej*, jumping and dancing with the instrument. Inside the hut, Sia was watching, distracted, mesmerized by his passion and skill. Meanwhile, the pot of boiling rice was simmering over. Rice grains overflowed on the side of the pot and nearly put out the fire underneath. The burnt smell snapped Sia back to her task. She rushed to rescue the pot of boiling rice, and met a cloud of dark steam.

"You burnt the food. You're not my wife," said Xai. He stood at the doorway, judging her. *Sia wouldn't have burned the food.*

Of all the things she had been through, it was the disappointment on her husband's face right now that hurt the most. Sia stammered, "I can make it again." There was desperation in her voice. "I'll be more careful this time."

He watched her closely the second time. Sia was meticulous with every step of cooking. She stirred the pot of simmering rice occasionally and seasoned the boiled chicken perfectly with herbs and spices.

An hour later, Xai sat in a wooden chair at the table, admiring the simple, hot meal. He took the bowl of boiled chicken and sipped from the brim. The flavors of fresh chicken broth, wild herbs, and salt touched his tongue. His cheeks were flushed with warmth and delight. The sweet and delicate texture of the soft steaming rice in his mouth pleased him. It satisfied Xai. He smiled and offered Sia a bowl of rice.

For Sia, the trust had always been there, but she was glad that her husband had put his trust in her again—even if it was just over a well-cooked meal. She asked him, "Were you afraid that something else may have returned instead of your wife?"

"Forgive me, but I am certain now that my wife has returned to me." Xai reached for her hand. "I'm glad you're home."

"I'm glad to be home."

"Where's your horse?"

"He found a new home, with others like him," said Sia. "So I let him go."

He squeezed her hand, a little surprised she was able to let go of the horse.

"I know you loved him," said Xai.

It was true, she did love the horse as much as any human can love another. He was family. She was silent. Xai poured a cup of tea and offered it to her. She gladly took the hot cup from him with a smile. He smiled back. The couple dined together, celebrating their reunion silently, with joy on their faces.

CHAPTER 17
HMONG NEW YEAR

The pleasant noise of people gathered in cheerful crowds. Hot meals sizzling from dozens of food shops. The thin fog fading in the warm sunlight. It was welcomed by all, young and old. The Hmong New Year happened every winter. People bundled up in warm, silky gowns, fine coats, elaborate hats, and bold silver necklaces. Shy young men and women met for the first time, courting one another.

Xai and Sia entered the crowded street, which had shops lining each side. They wore matching colored outfits and silver spirit locks. Sia's deep forest-green dress was covered in hand-embroidered designs that mirrored the stitched symbols on Xai's sleeves. They ate sweet and savory dishes from humble cooks. Sia did a double-take at a jewelry shop on the corner. Everything in the shop was marvelous and silver.

Xai took notice, and suggested to his wife, "Would you like some new jewelry to go with your new dress?"

"I don't have a new dress."

Xai replied charmingly, "Then today would be a good day to get a few new dresses."

"It'd be rude of me to refuse such a generous offer," Sia teased him, half-jokingly.

He admired her beauty. Her face had healed well from the wounds she acquired recently. There were no visible scars. He stared at the perfect skin on her face.

"Is something wrong?" asked Sia.

"Your wounds are all healed. It's as if you never had them," said Xai, a little curious, but grateful.

"I was afraid my face would be scarred."

"You would still be beautiful." His words made her glad, and she smiled.

Three well-dressed men waved to them with friendly faces. Sia recognized the group of friendly men. "Old friends of yours."

Xai waved back to them. "Yes. They came to our wedding. Do you remember the groomsman?"

"Yes, the scared one," Sia recalled.

"He won't let me leave without a drink."

"I'll take my time at the jewelry shop then."

Xai smiled at her. "Don't be too long. Come and save me from drinking too much. I don't feel as young as them anymore."

"I shall try, husband." Sia went forward as her husband joined his old friends. She entered the sparkling jewelry shop. Everything was made from silver. Fine silver necklaces were on display, along with spirit locks and elaborate neck pieces. Some items were embedded with rich crystals and gemstones.

The shop owner was talking to a mother and daughter; both women had powdered faces, rosy cheeks, and red lips. Their clothes were vibrant, made out of the finest fabrics.

"These items look new," said the daughter.

"Yes, Pa," the shop owner said to the daughter. "They are new." She greeted another set of new customers with a smile. The new customers were three young girls wearing their brightest and newest dresses. But none present in the building compared to the shop owner. Her black gown had pearls sewn on the sleeves and hems of the dress. She wore large silver hairpins that complemented her long, dark hair, and the necklace around her neck had more class and style than anything else that was for sale. She looked like royalty, and even walked like it.

Pa announced, "Have you heard? I'm married." The proud young girl of only fifteen years old walked slowly down the aisle of dazzling silver headpieces, touching them with her fat fingers.

"Yes. I'm happy for you, sister Pa," said the shop owner.

Pa proudly replied, "Thank you. Forgive me. I didn't invite you. I hope you're not upset with me, Lee."

"No, I'm not upset," replied Lee, the shop owner. Her voice had a sense of calm and class.

Sia's eyes were dazzled by the earring and ring sections. She looked back to check on her husband, who was smiling and chattering among the group of young men.

"And when will you get married, Lee?" asked Pa's mother, with her nose in the air.

That comment got the awkward attention of all the women in the shop.

"Not soon," Lee answered confidently.

"You're getting old for a maid," said Pa's mother.

"I'm twenty-two," Lee replied.

"Exactly. You're an old maid. Perhaps my cousin's son will marry you. He's looking for a wife."

"The new year is full of girls," said Lee, trying to be respectful. "I'm sure he'll find someone. I'm—"

Pa's mother quickly cut Lee off with, "He's blind. He needs a resourceful wife who can help him." She was pushy. "Like you."

She had crossed the line. Lee couldn't stop herself. "Perhaps you can marry him. You have two dead husbands," said Lee. "Which makes you very resourceful." The other customers giggled and left the shop in a hurry.

Pa's mother's face flushed with red from the embarrassment. "Let's go to another shop, Pa. I won't buy anything here." She stormed off with her head held high. Pa followed behind her demanding mother like the clueless child that she was.

"I apologize for that," Lee said with a little embarrassment.

"What a shameless woman. There's others like her," Sia said light-heartedly. "We can't be angry. So should we laugh instead?" She chuckled.

Lee laughed too. "Do you see anything that you like?"

"I like everything here," said Sia. "Do you know why all the spirit locks are made of silver?"

"Silver has many properties and purposes, such as protection from harmful spirits."

"Yes, I'm sure it's not just a tall tale," said Sia.

"There's truth in every tale," Lee agreed.

"That's wise." Sia touched the set of rings. "Everything here is silver?"

"Real silver. I never use anything less."

Sia picked up a lovely, thin silver comb.

"I'll take this one. You made all of these?"

"Yes, I did." Lee started to explain. "I know it's a man's trade, but we don't have sons in our family. And silver is my family's trade."

Lee put the silver comb that Sia picked out into a wooden box lined with cloth.

"Everything in here is fit for a queen. No other shop or merchant can compare to the detail and beauty I see here."

"Here." Lee took out a tray containing a set of matching earrings, necklace, bracelets, and hairpins. "My newest work."

Sia fell instantly in love with the finely crafted silver jewelry set. "They're beautiful. I'll purchase all of them," she said.

Then her eyes caught the sight of the gold ring on Lee's hand. She recognized the diamond-shaped seal on the alluring piece. A wave of darkness washed over the crown of her head and took away her joy. All her fears had returned.

Lee noticed Sia staring at her ring, and said, "It's not for sale."

"Where did you get this ring?"

"It's a family heirloom."

"Is there more than one ring, like this one?"

"You've seen this ring before?" Lee said suspiciously.

"Yes."

"Where?"

"On a dead woman."

Lee was shocked. "How?"

"I apologize if I'm scaring you."

"I'm not scared. I'm concerned."

"Concerned? So, there is another ring like this one."

Lee stayed quiet. *Yes.* She didn't have to answer, it was on her face.

"I have questions, and I will answer any questions you have. I know it seems impossible to see the dead. I have and…" Sia quickly looked to her husband outside. "He has."

Lee replied with, "It's possible. A lot of things are possible."

"Please tell me about the other ring."

"That is a long story."

Sia looked over her shoulder to check that her husband was still catching up with his friends. The men were now toasting each other with drinks now. "I have the time."

"I guess I can close the shop for a short while," said Lee. "Thank you."

Lee grabbed the red ropes from either side of the door and tied them together with a sign hanging in the middle. She led Sia to a nearby table and lifted the cover from a tray of colorful, sticky desserts. Lee filled two silver cups with the clear liquid from a silver vase and offered a cup to Sia.

Sia set the wooden box aside, accepted the cup, and said, "Thank you." She held the cup towards her lips, and smelled the strong, sweet scent of wine.

"It's rice wine," said Lee before gulping down the drink in her hand.

Rice wine. Sia knew it was better to consume the drink as quickly as possible, and she shot it into her mouth. The rice wine burned her tongue and the inside of her cheeks, and traveled up her nose, all within a second. She swallowed, and it stung down her throat. The hot sensation stayed on her tongue. There was still a small amount left at the bottom of the cup. She made a bitter face before finishing the rest of the drink.

Lee refilled their cups and said, "I'm Mai Lee. The villagers just call me Lee after my great-great-great-great-great-great-great-great-great grandmother." She counted with all her fingers. Sia almost burst out in laughter, but she contained herself.

"She lived more than a century ago, and she was the first woman to make and sell silver here. Every one of my family members who owned this shop at one time was named after her. I just call her great-grandmother Lee. What's your name?"

"I'm the wife of Xai."

"Xai and Sia?" Lee had heard of them.

"Yes."

Lee looked delighted to meet Sia.

"Since you're here, I must ask you," said Lee. "What possessed you to go into the dark world for your dead husband? No one I know would ever do such a foolish thing."

"I thought only the villagers knew. How did you hear about us?"

"You answer my question first, and then I will gladly answer yours."

Sia took a moment, and then said, "Perhaps one day, you will discover how far you are willing to go for someone you love."

"That does not answer my question, and you make falling in love sound dangerous," said Lee. "I'm not in a hurry to marry, and I'm content with my own company. So, tell me, what was the scariest thing you've encountered on your journeys?"

Sia took a moment. It was not the underworld and the creatures that scared her the most. "Loneliness scared me more than anything I had encountered before."

"More than the dark world? More than spirits, and monsters?" asked Lee.

Sia firmly believed it. "Yes."

"You surprise me."

Lee saw the way Sia was looking at her, waiting on her.

"To answer your question from earlier," said Lee. "Shamans talk, and my entire family are shamans. Some of them are in denial, and others are praising your story." Lee raised her cup to Sia. "Here's to you."

"Thank you." Sia raised her cup to Lee. They both drank.

"That's strong. And good." Sia gave her compliments after emptying her cup.

Lee stuffed her mouth with desserts, speaking with a full mouth, "Have some sweets."

"Perhaps later. Thank you," said Sia.

Lee refilled her cup and reached over to Sia's cup.

Sia covered the rim of her cup. "I don't drink often."

"Are you sure your husband won't be looking for you?" Lee asked.

"He can spend hours with his friends," Sia assured her.

"It's the new year, people will celebrate." Lee sounded a little annoyed by the holiday. She looked at Sia and then to the gold ring. "Are you sure you want to know about this cursed thing?"

"Yes."

Lee sighs. "Open your mind and your heart. Families have told our history like a ghost story, but I think it's a tragic love story." Her tone grew serious. "I suppose I should start at the beginning."

Lee slipped off the gold ring, showing it to Sia. "There are only two of these rings that exist," said Lee. The ring was alluring, as if it were enchanted. Sia was tempted to touch it, but she stopped herself, holding her hands in her lap.

"It calls to you, doesn't it? I've learned to shut it out of my mind," said Lee. She put the ring back on her finger, and Sia instantly felt less drawn to it.

"Our ancestor, Pa Kou, went on a journey to seek a healer for her sick children. Instead, she became lost in the woods and took shelter in a cave. There she met an ancient spirit, who gave her two rings to pass onto her children. *It will save them*, the spirit told her. But in return, they will be tied to the spirit in life and in death." Lee took a drink. This part was always hard to believe. "The spirit wanted two brides from this family. It was willing to wait until someone chose to marry it. Pa Kou returned home with the gold rings, and her children were saved as promised. Then strange things began to happen, she saw spirits and was able to speak to them. She lost time in the night and in the mornings, traveling to the spirit world. She traveled so far into the dark world that she met the ancient spirit from the cave again. Only this time, she was in its world. The ancient spirit taught her many things, and gave her gifts before she left his realm. When she returned to the world of the living, her daughters had died of old age."

Sia was saddened by that part of the story, and Lee took notice.

Lee continued, "She had been gone so long that even her grandchildren and great-grandchildren, who were all women, had died. She collected the rings from the graves of her daughters and gave them to the next of kin, who happened to have twin daughters. She taught the twins strange ceremonies. One of the daughters had a broken heart after running away with an already-married man. She was wronged in the saddest way for a young girl, so, out of vengeance, she conjured the ancient spirit and offered to marry it in return for the power to create curses and take men. The day after they found her body, Pa Kou warned the family about their daughter who married a demon. Then Pa Kou walked into the woods and was never seen again. The other twin was the one I call great-grandmother Lee."

"That is a tragic love story."

"Yes, for great-grandmother Lee's sister."

"For Pa Kou."

Lee didn't seem to understand what she meant.

"She was so desperate to save her children, that she accidentally cursed them."

"No one has ever said that before," said Lee, surprised.

"Every one of her kin after the trade was born a woman. It was as if the ancient spirit made it so that it can have brides."

"And tragedies followed," said Lee. "One after another. Misfortune skips a generation sometimes."

Sia sympathized with her. "Perhaps we all carry a curse of our own."

"Then we all have something in common."

"Do you believe in it?" asked Sia.

"The story? Or the ring?"

"All of it."

"I'm definitely afraid of what the ring represents."

"I've heard stories about Pa Kou, the second most powerful shaman of her time. She created a family of gifted shamans," said Sia. "You're from the second family of shamans, which is a very well-known and respected family."

"Yes, so they say."

"You're part of a very powerful family."

"I do not feel powerful," said Lee. "And the second family is falling apart, becoming divided. Power can do that. I will never rely on my gifts like they do. That is why I'm not really a part of the second family. I've seen what magic, dark magic, can do to a family, and I will never pass it on to my children."

"If what you say is true, then your ancestor was among the dead that took my husband. If she is that powerful, then I was lucky to bring him back."

"Perhaps the gods favor you."

"Are gods real?"

"Why not? Spirits are."

"I cannot disagree."

"Perhaps you are a descendent of the first family," said Lee, deep in thought. "You must have heard of them. The very first shaman created the first family of gifted people. They're legends compared to mine, and far superior when it comes to dealing with spirits and magic."

It was hard for Sia to believe she'd come from such a mysterious and famous family. She chuckled. "I was born in a small village. I've never met my grandparents. I don't know much about spirits or silver."

"A woman who can enter the world of the dead and bring her deceased husband back to life," Lee said, and paused to sip from her third cup of rice wine. "Seems like a very gifted shaman to me." She poured herself another drink. "Are you certain you don't want one?"

Sia lifted her cup to Lee. There was a hint of satisfaction on Lee's face as she filled Sia's cup.

Sia brought the conversation back to the story. "Your ancestor, the one that married a demon. What was her name? Tell me about her."

"I must warn you, she'll never leave your husband."

"Why?"

"Well, she took your husband once, she will eventually take him again. And it's part of her curse."

"How do I stop her?"

"You cannot," Lee's tone was serious. "Ever heard of something darker than evil spirits? Demons."

"No, but I may have met one. I'm not sure." Sia asked, "Will you tell the story of the demon bride? I want to know more about her."

"Before she became a demon bride, she was called Mai Neng, and she was in love with a man. It was over a thousand years ago."

CHAPTER 18
THE SPIRITS RETURNED

Black. It was the rich color of the steaming tea in Sia's cup. The image of Neng's dead body in the center of the divided black tree, with pale blue skin, and black lips haunted Sia's thoughts like a black bird repeating the same line as though it was stuck in a time loop. Some hours had passed by this time, and she was still in the silver jewelry shop with Lee. Empty wine vases and the cups used for wine sat to the side.

"She performed the one ceremony that our elders forbade us to do. She became a demon bride. She's cursed," said Lee. There was sadness in her words. "But you may be right; we're all cursed somehow."

Sia snapped back to reality. "I can't help but feel sympathy for her. Is that wrong of me to pity my enemy?" asked Sia.

"It is hard not to pity her," said Lee.

Sia sipped the hot black tea. It became quiet and awkward in the shop.

Lee wanted to break the silence. "But she did take your husband, which meant she probably caused his death." She said light-heartedly, "While you were in the dark world, she may have thought of killing you as well. She has become your enemy. She does not deserve your sympathy." The two women smiled. Lee topped off their cups with hot tea. "Are you sure you don't want more wine?"

"Yes," said Sia, as she took the hot cup from the table. She suddenly had a curious thought. "What happened to that man, Blong?"

"He fell sick. People said he claimed to be haunted by an old lover." Lee let out a small chuckle. "He went mad with his illness for a year. Then one day, he died in his sleep."

"There's many stories eerily similar to that one, today."

"Exactly, but some say she's just a story."

"Like you said earlier, perhaps every story has some form of truth within it," Sia said. "My experience has shown me that I should start believing in everything, especially if it is *just a story*."

That put a smile on Lee's face. "I suppose, someday, all we will be are stories."

"It is comforting to know we'll be remembered," said Sia, quoting her husband.

Xai approached the silver shop and Lee saw him arriving. "Keep your husband close," she advised Sia.

Sia looked to the door and found her husband standing there, waiting with a warm smile. She stood up and thanked Lee.

"Thank you for the wine and the tea." Sia took the wrapped boxes of jewelry into her arms.

"Thank you for spending a lot in my shop," said Lee.

The women both gave each other their respects as they stood up and faced each other to say goodbye.

"You're welcome to come back any time." Lee sounded sincere. She wished Sia well, "Safe journey."

Sia said kindly, "Let us meet again."

Touched, Lee replied, "Let us meet again." She reopened the shop and stepped aside for Sia to leave.

Sia joined her husband at the door. The two left the shop together, stepping into the cold winter air. Then Sia spotted someone in the crowd, and stopped her in her tracks; it was the demon bride.

Xai noticed his wife had stopped walking. "What's wrong?" The demon bride vanished into the crowded market.

Sia shook it off. "I thought I saw…someone I knew."

"Who?"

Sia didn't want to scare him. "I was mistaken."

They continued into the market. Xai took her hand, trying to keep it warm, and it made Sia feel safe. The busy markets drowned out her fears for a moment.

Months had passed. The season grew warm again. Things were back to normal. Harvesting in the garden. Feeding the livestock. Hot baths under the moonlight. Meals by candlelight. Stories in bed with damp hair. Life was good again. This perfect life went on for many days.

However, there was one small problem. Late into the night while Xai slept, his wife struggled to close her eyes. The voices of spirits disturbed her. Non-stop chattering that came from the wall behind their bed. Angry words, cursing and blaming Sia for all that had happened. Every night, the whispers would begin the moment Xai closed his eyes and continued to the moment he opened them. This supernatural situation carried on for weeks, which felt like months for Sia. The dark circles under her eyes grew larger and darker with each sleepless night, while her husband remained oblivious and unaffected. Sia realized she was the only one who could hear the spirits. The dead were taunting her once more, stealing her sleep.

Enough. Sia came up with a clever idea. It was a ritual that her father had once done in secret—not knowing that there had been a ten-year-old witness. The hour had been late at night, and everyone in the house was asleep, except for them. The blazing fireplace cast long shadows over the floor. Little Sia stood quietly in the doorway of the living room, watching the rare sight of her father perform old magic by the fire. He was chanting a spell, and it sounded like poetry.

Back in the present, Sia heated stones in the fireplace and enchanted them, whispering her commands to the fire. She laid the scorching stones outside along the wall where the bed rested. That night, Sia watched Xai fall asleep. She stayed alert, listening to the wall.

Along came the spirits. They settled on the outside of the wall. Sizzling noises came first. Instead of cursing words, the spirits were shouting in pain. The smell of burning ashes flowed through the cracks of the bamboo wall. The hot stones had burnt the spirits at their bottoms and feet. Panicked spirits dispersed and soon it became quiet on the property.

The spirits drifted into the pitch-black woods. Among them in the dark was the demon bride. She was waiting and watching their house patiently. The spirits all gathered on a hill where they could see the couple's hut at the edge of the village. The grisly spirits shouted loudly as one, "You dare be so bold to keep Xai? Then live to old age with him. Never curse at him or wish for death, because the day you speak the words, Xai will die and he will be ours forever. You will never get him back."

Those words echoed through all the walls of the little hut, sending a surge of dark vibration through the ground. Sia heard the spirits. They had warned her.

Sia faced her husband. His calm, content expression grounded her back into the safety of their home. She held him, and he felt her warm body.

Xai softly spoke, "Sleep, wife."

"Xai?"

"Yes?" He was half awake with his eyes closed.

"Don't leave me again."

"Never."

Sia closed her eyes.

CHAPTER 19
WORDS

For months, Sia was careful with her words.

One evening, Sia let down her hair and took the silver crafted comb from the table of hair accessories. Xai approached behind her and took the comb from her. He finely brushed through Sia's long, dark hair. He found a single white hair among her dark strands; it was a sign of aging, and it humbled him to be able to age with her.

Xai told her, "You have beautiful hair."

"Thank you, husband," said Sia.

The couple sat by the fire and shared a bottle of rice wine. Sia refilled her husband's bowl with more rice wine and asked, "How's the rice wine?"

"Delicious," replied Xai.

For years, she had only used kind words towards Xai as she had always done before. Sia finished sewing a new robe. She helped Xai get dressed for a festive event. Their hut was decorated with fresh flowers and gifts, and filled with an abundance of food: fresh fruits, meat, and grains. The pleasant commotion of folks passing by in their finest attire could be seen from the open windows. A little boy and girl, both around ten years old, chased each other outside. Seeing them made Sia secretly long for children.

The children's mothers shouted their names.

"Pheng!"

"Mai!"

The children immediately ran to their mothers, and everyone went on their way to the festival.

Xai and Sia were good to each other. With time, unpleasant memories became lost in the past. The bad chapters of their lives seemed far away and almost non-existent. They were living an ordinary life, and they were happy. Harmonious. There were ten perfect years together.

One day, Sia was preparing dinner, and she looked out the window to see a young man and young woman carrying baskets of vegetables. They were teenagers, and flirtatious. Their mothers were coming to meet them, and called out their names.

"Pheng!"

"Mai."

The children went to their mothers. Sia returned to her work, slicing bitter melons on a round, flat wooden block. Xai entered their home with a basket of firewood and a wrapped gift in one hand. Sia's face lit up. They were all each other needed.

Then, one day, their lives changed a second time. It happened early in the morning. The sky was a dark blue, bursting with yellow and white from the sun. A strange haze began to sweep the land, and the spirits returned to the edge of the woods. They were watching the village, watching Xai and Sia's home.

Inside the hut, Xai was still sleeping in bed while Sia brushed her hair with the silver comb she bought from Lee. *Crack.* The silver comb broke in half and cut two of her fingers. She set the broken comb down and looked at the minor cuts. Sia grabbed the nearest cloth and held it around her bleeding fingers. Clashing pots drew Sia's attention to the other end of the hut. There was a chicken running around in the kitchen, knocking over pots and bowls. The brown-feathered bird stayed at the fireplace. The wood was nearly burnt out, but it was still glowing red and hot in the center. Sia ushered the chicken away and opened the front door, but the chicken clucked around and circled right back to the fireplace, leaving a trail of tipped-over bowls and food supplies. The bird beat its wings at Sia's face, and it jumped out of her hands. The noise woke Xai. He sat up and locked eyes with Sia. Her hair was a mess. She sighed with an embarrassed expression.

It was warm outside, so Sia didn't understand why the chicken kept squatting at the fireplace. She tried to chase the chicken out the door again, but it wouldn't leave. The chicken flapped over Sia and landed back at the fireplace. Feathers in the air, feathers everywhere. Frustrated, Sia said, "Curse you to death!"

Right away, Xai felt pain in his chest. There was a hand there at his heart with dark long fingernails and a gold ring. Frightened, he exhaled. His sight was fading. He stood up, but his legs couldn't hold him. Xai gathered all his strength to call, "Sia…"

At the sound of her name, Sia turned just in time to see her husband drop toward the ground. Behind him stood the demon bride, smiling with black lips, satisfied at last.

The windows burst open and a dark wind blasted into the home. Sia's long hair flew into her face. It was only a second before Sia could see again, but the vengeful spirit was gone from the scene.

Crash! Xai hit the floor on his side. He saw his wife rushing to him in a panic.

Sia cried out his name, "Xai!"

Xai shut his eyes. His heart stopped. Darkness.

Back in the world of the living, Sia was alone as she sat next to her deceased husband. His body decomposed rapidly, rotting within the hour. It was an unnatural thing to happen. Sia gathered flowers and laid them out around his body to mask the awful scent. By noon, she noticed the complete physical change. Her husband no longer looked like himself anymore: instead, he was a decayed corpse.

There was a second funeral for Xai. It was uncommon. People only died once. Yet Sia buried her husband again. There was a small group of people at the burial site. Only immediate family and relatives attended the service this time. The pink flowers covered the grave beautifully, but the horrible smell coming from deep inside the grave still caused people to cover their mouths and noses. When it was over and everyone had gone home, Sia waited at Xai's grave. She gave him all the things he had asked for from the first death, such as his instruments and a hot meal. She stayed by his grave for days, but he never rose again. Heartbroken, starving, and dying, she surrendered still resting on his grave. Her will to live withered like the dying pink flowers around her. She wanted to follow him. Her breath was shallow.

Tears filled her tired eyes. This could be the end for her; she felt it in her bones.

Suddenly, a shadow fell over her.

"Daughter." It was the voice of the divine goddess.

"You…" Sia recognized that angelic voice. She barely had the strength to speak, "Have you come to take me?"

"Rise, daughter," said a deep calming voice. The shadow figure transformed to an older man, someone familiar. His voice sounded like home.

"Father?" Sia knew him. "Help me."

"I have," replied the shadow man that resembled the shape of Sia's father.

"Help me save my husband," Sia pleaded.

"You have already saved me." Now it was Xai's kind voice. The shadow became Xai. "Now save yourself." He was a jet-black silhouette inside a vignette, with a halo of light tracing his figure.

Weak, Sia tried to lift her hand to touch the shadow, but she failed. Her frail fingers trembled in the dirt. "What was it all for, if we can't be together?"

"Wherever you go, I'll go, too," said Xai.

His sweet voice put her heart at ease. The frame around her vision grew dark and bled into the shadows. Sia was alone again. Her heartbeat was faint, and her vision faded to pitch-black.

The rushing water fell off the edges of the rooftop and pitter-pattered on the ground outside. The calm melody of rainfall woke Sia up. She could see the roof of the hut. It was her home. She lay in bed, overwhelmed and drained. The cool air rushed in from the open window, bringing a light mist onto her skin.

Sia rose from the bed, her head weighing heavier than she could normally manage. Pink flowers fell into her lap. She touched the side of her head, and found another pink flower. She stared at the delicate flowers in her dirty palms. There was dirt on her dress and dirt at her feet.

Everything was real. Sia knew she had not dreamed of speaking to spirits, and the last one was her husband. A flicker of hope crossed her mind.

It was the thought of Xai's last words. "Wherever you go, I'll go, too."

Sia repeated, "Wherever you go, I'll go, too."

A roar of thunder clapped above the hut.

CHAPTER 20
SHAMANS

Sia was still holding the pink flowers in her hand. "Wherever you go, I'll go, too." It had been a long day after the burial in the morning.

Thunder rolled above the hut, and lightning lit up the sky outside: white, then dark again. The land suddenly grew darker. The livestock panicked and ran for shelter. A second thunderclap rumbled, followed by two alarming knocks at the front door.

Sia went to answer the knocking. She opened the door to an elderly couple, a desperate-looking man with strange tools in one hand, and a pale woman standing beside him. Both of them were soaked from the rain, and their noses were bright red. Sia felt sympathy for them.

"Hello," said the elderly man.

"Hello," replied Sia.

He sneezed, and then said, "We're just passing through. My wife has a fever. She's unable to travel. We need shelter…and food." He looked ashamed.

Sia quickly scanned the couple. The elderly man was carrying tools, but nothing harmful. Lightning flashed behind them, highlighting the haunted woods. A forceful wind followed the thunder. Everyone shivered.

The elderly man quickly said, "We've been turned down twice in this town. I have no silver, but I can work." He sounded earnest. "I'll do any kind of work you ask of me."

"What kind of work can you do?" Sia clearly saw that the couple were not fit for hard labor at their age. It would be cruel to make them.

"Our work deals with the spiritual realm, but we also grow our own food and raise cattle back at home. I'm skilled at welding metal tools like this one," said the elderly man, holding up a large metal ring with silver coins hanging around it. Something in her face caught the old man's eye. He stared at her for a moment, with a knowing expression. "You're no stranger to spirits."

Sia was interested. "What exactly are your dealings with the spiritual realm?"

"We're shamans," answered the elderly man. He looked to his wife, who seemed to be in worse shape than before. "My wife travels to the underworld to deal with spirits. She can speak to spirits of all forms," he informed Sia with pride, "And I ferry the souls of the dead."

"For funerals," said Sia.

She took them for common shamans, and the old man heard it in her voice.

"We are not common shamans." The old man was calm, but there was authority in his voice. "I'm from the first family of shamans, and my wife is a descendant of the second family of shamans. Our magic is the oldest kind, and far from common."

"I apologize, I meant no offense."

The old woman lost her balance. Sia caught the old woman by her arm. The old man held up his wife.

"Help us, and I will return the favor," the old man promised. "We shamans are bound by our words."

Sia wouldn't turn them away in this condition. "Please come inside," she said, pushing the door wide open.

The elderly shaman couple entered the hut and went straight to the warm fireplace. Sia shut the door behind them. Then she took a set of blankets from the storage chest, and gave them to the elderly couple.

"Thank you," said the old man. He reached for the blankets and touched her fingers, which gave him a vision. It was a quick glimpse of Sia eating snails in the dark world, and spirits of the dead surrounded her. The vision quickly faded. The old man stared at Sia briefly, and a dark feeling shot through him like a lightning bolt of destructive energy. He turned to his wife for answers and saw that she was still shivering. He quickly wrapped her with one blanket, and then he bundled up with the other one.

"Would you both like some tea?" asked Sia, as she poured hot water over tea leaves at a small, square table near the fire.

"Yes." The old man shivered. He looked at his wife, she appeared to be doing better than before. The fire felt good on their wrinkled skin and warmed their numb hands and faces.

She offered a tray with two steaming cups of tea to the elderly couple. They drank and held the hot cups in their hands to keep them warm. The aroma of green tea leaves, lemongrass, and fresh ginger was soothing. The old woman breathed in the therapeutic steam from her cup; it smelled like home to her, and her tensed shoulders relaxed. Sia sipped from her cup and gave them a moment to enjoy the tea.

"Have you heard of the demon bride?" asked Sia.

The mention of that name shocked the old man.

"Yes," he replied.

"I heard she cannot be stopped," said Sia.

The old man paused, wondering if he should answer her. Then he spotted the broom that hung by the side of the door. *She may be more like them then she realized.* He replied, "You heard wrong. Even demons can be defeated, cast out, banished, and locked away."

"How does one accomplish that?"

"Why would you want to do something so dangerous?"

"For the sake of my husband's soul."

The elderly couple looked at each other. *What had they gotten themselves into?*

The old man told Sia, "There are terrible things in the dark world. More horror than anyone can imagine. Maybe you already know. I've heard about you, Sia. That is your name, isn't it?"

Sia appeared surprised that he knew her. She nodded to him with a friendly smile.

"I've heard that those who eat or drink from the dark world will come back different, that is *if* they return at all," said the old man.

It took Sia a moment to figure out that he was talking about her. She remembered eating the snails and worms in the dark world. She looked down, trying to collect her thoughts before saying something. Then Sia noticed that the recent cuts on fingers had healed without a trace of injury, but she hadn't noticed that before. *Perhaps the shaman was right. And perhaps her chances are better this time.* "I heard that shamans are bound by their words," said Sia, repeating the old man's words from earlier. "I would like that favor soon, please."

The old woman nodded to her husband.

The old man held up the cup of tea and asked, "Do you have something stronger?"

A hopeful smile crossed Sia's face. She was excited for all the things that were possible.

The sharp, loud crack of thunder clashed over the hut. The storm was directly above them.

The end…for now.

Let us meet again.

ABOUT THE AUTHOR

Bao Xiong is the founder of Moth House Press, an indie publishing house focused on dark genres, folklore, non-traditional and female lead stories. Bao was born in Thailand in a refugee camp. Her family, like many Hmong families from Laos, were involved in the Secret War during the Vietnam War. They migrated to the U.S. in the late 80's. She majored in Visual Communications and pursues a career in literature and media.

For more books from this author, please visit:
https://www.mothhouse.org/books